Edgar Wallace was born illegitimate
adopted by George Freeman, a porter
eleven, Wallace sold newspapers at Ludgate Circus and on leaving
school took a job with a printer. He enlisted in the Royal West Kent
Regiment, later transferring to the Medical Staff Corps, and was sent
to South Africa. In 1898 he published a collection of poems called
The Mission that Failed, left the army and became a correspondent
for Reuters.

Wallace became the South African war correspondent for *The
Daily Mail*. His articles were later published as *Unofficial Dispatches* and
his outspokenness infuriated Kitchener, who banned him as a war
correspondent until the First World War. He edited the *Rand Daily
Mail*, but gambled disastrously on the South African Stock Market,
returning to England to report on crimes and hanging trials. He
became editor of *The Evening News*, then in 1905 founded the Tallis
Press, publishing *Smithy*, a collection of soldier stories, and *Four Just
Men*. At various times he worked on *The Standard*, *The Star*, *The Week-
End Racing Supplement* and *The Story Journal*.

In 1917 he became a Special Constable at Lincoln's Inn and also
a special interrogator for the War Office. His first marriage to Ivy
Caldecott, daughter of a missionary, had ended in divorce and he
married his much younger secretary, Violet King.

The Daily Mail sent Wallace to investigate atrocities in the Belgian
Congo, a trip that provided material for his *Sanders of the River* books.
In 1923 he became Chairman of the Press Club and in 1931 stood as
a Liberal candidate at Blackpool. On being offered a scriptwriting
contract at RKO, Wallace went to Hollywood. He died in 1932, on
his way to work on the screenplay for *King Kong*.

BY THE SAME AUTHOR
ALL PUBLISHED BY HOUSE OF STRATUS

The Man who
was Nobody

HOUSE OF
STRATUS

This edition published in 2001 by House of Stratus, an imprint of
Stratus Books Ltd., 21 Beeching Park, Kelly Bray,
Cornwall, PL17 8QS, UK.

www.houseofstratus.com

Typeset, printed and bound by House of Stratus.

A catalogue record for this book is available from the British Library
and the Library of Congress.

ISBN 07551-150-8-2

We would like to thank the Edgar Wallace Society for all the support they have given
House of Stratus. Enquiries on how to join the Edgar Wallace Society should be addressed to:
The Edgar Wallace Society, c/o Penny Wyrd, 84 Ridgefield Road, Oxford, OX4 3DA.
Email: info@edgarwallace.org Web: http://www.edgarwallace.org/

CONTENTS

Contents (contd)

AT ALMA'S FLAT

"Well, you've got him! What do you think of him?"

Augustus Javot's thin lips were twisted in a cynical smile as he surveyed the scene. The small drawing-room was in confusion, the furniture had been pushed against the wall in order to give the dancers a little more room. One electric wall bracket had been twisted out of shape by a drunken hand, and a great bowl of white lilac had been smashed and now lay upon the floor in a confusion of broken china and wilted blooms. At one end of the room a mechanical piano tinkled metallically and half a dozen couples swayed through the motion of a two-step with unsteady feet amidst a babble of raucous laughter and half-hysterical giggles.

The handsome girl who stood by Javot's side let her eyes wander about the apartment till they rested upon a flushed youth who was at that moment endeavouring to stand on his hands against the wall, encouraged thereto by the ear-piercing cat-calls of one who was scarcely less sober than the amateur acrobat.

Alma Trebizond raised her eyebrows never so slightly and turned to meet Javot's gaze.

"Beggars can't be choosers," she said complacently. "He isn't very impressive, but he is a baronet of the United Kingdom and has a rent-roll of forty thousand a year."

"And the Tynewood diamond collar," murmured Javot. "It will be a new thing to see you with a hundred thousand pounds of diamonds round your pretty neck, my dear."

The girl fetched a long sigh, the sigh of one who has dared much and has succeeded beyond her wildest hopes.

"It has turned out better than I expected," she said, and then: "I have sent an announcement to the papers."

Javot looked at her sharply. He was a thin, hard-faced man, slightly bald, and there was a hawk-like look in his cold eyes as he surveyed her unsmilingly.

"You've sent to the papers?" he said slowly. "I think you're a bit of a fool, Alma!"

"Why?" she asked defiantly. "I've nothing to be ashamed of – I'm as good as he is! Besides, it's not unusual for an actress of my ability to marry into the peerage."

"It's not exactly the peerage," corrected Javot, "but that's beside the point. He's particularly asked you to keep the marriage secret."

"Why should I?" she demanded.

A little smile twinkled in his eyes.

"There are many reasons," he said significantly, "and I could give you one if it were necessary. You're not going to send the announcement to the papers, Alma."

"I've already done it," she replied sullenly.

He made a little impatient noise.

"You're starting badly," he said. "Sir James Tynewood was not drunk when he asked you to keep the marriage a secret for twelve months. He was particularly sober, Alma, and he had a reason, you may be sure."

With an impatient shrug she turned from him and walked across to the balancing youth who was now on his feet holding in a shaky hand a champagne glass which his companion was endeavouring to fill, with disastrous results to Alma's drawing-room carpet.

"I want you, Jimmie," she said, and linked her arm in the young man's.

He turned a flushed smiling face towards her.

"Wait a minute, darling," he said thickly. "I'm just going to have another glass with dear old Mark."

"You're coming along with me for a moment," she insisted, and with a chuckle he dropped the glass to the floor, shivering it into a hundred pieces.

"I'm married now, eh?" he chuckled. "Got to obey the wife!"

She led him back to where Javot stood. "Jimmie," she said suddenly, "I've sent the announcement of our wedding to the papers."

He stared at her in drunken amazement and a frown gathered on his forehead.

"Say that again," he repeated.

"I've sent the announcement that Alma Trebizond, the eminent actress, has married Sir James Tynewood, of Tynewood Chase," she said coolly. "I'm not going to have any secrecy about this business, Jimmie. You're not ashamed of me?"

He had drawn his arm from hers and stood, the frown still upon his face, his hand rumpling his hair in an effort of thought.

"I told you not to," he said with sudden violence. "Damn it, didn't I tell you not to, Alma?"

And then suddenly his mood changed, and flinging back his head he roared with laughter.

"Well, that's the best thing I've heard," he gasped, wiping the tears of merriment from his eyes. "Come and have a drink, Javot."

But Augustus Javot shook his head.

"No, thank you, Sir James," he replied. "If you will take my advice – "

"Pshaw!" scorned the other. "I take nobody's advice in these days. I've taken Alma and that's all that matters, isn't it, darling?"

Javot watched him as he went across the room and shook his head.

"I wonder what his relations are going to say?" he asked softly.

The girl turned on him.

"Does it matter what his relations say?" she demanded. "Besides, he has no relations except a younger brother who's in America, and he's only a half-brother, anyway. What makes you so gloomy tonight, Javot?" she said irritably. "You're getting on my nerves."

Javot said nothing, but perched on the head of the sofa he watched the girl as she joined her husband and permitted himself to wonder what would be the end of the adventure. The merriment was at its height when a diversion came.

Alma's flat was in a fashionable block overlooking the park and the appearance of a servant in the doorway meant nothing more to Javot than that one of the tenants of the flats beneath had sent up complaints about the noise. It was the usual interruption to the gatherings which met in Alma's flat.

This time, however, the servant's message was important, for Alma signalled the company to silence, and the voice of Sir James was heard inquiring:

"For me?"

"Yes, sir," said the servant. "She wants to see you."

"Who is it?" asked Alma.

"A young woman, my lady," said the servant, who was training herself to address Alma in this unfamiliar style.

Alma laughed.

"Another of your conquests, Jimmie?" she said, and James Tynewood grinned sheepishly, for vanity was not the least of his vices.

"Bring her in," he said loudly, but the servant hesitated. "Bring her in," roared Tynewood, and the woman disappeared.

Presently she came back, followed by a girl, and at the sight of her Javot's eyes lightened.

"That's a pretty girl," he thought, and pretty indeed she was.

She looked round from one to the other of the company and she was obviously far from comfortable in those surroundings.

"Sir James Tynewood?" she asked in a soft voice.

"I'm Sir James Tynewood."

"I have a letter for you."

"For me?" repeated the other slowly. "Who the dickens have you come from?"

"From Vance & Vance," said the girl, and the face of Sir James Tynewood twitched.

"Oh you have, have you?" he said huskily.

Javot thought he detected a note of apprehension in the tone.

"I don't know why Mr Vance wants to bother me at this hour."

He took the letter from the girl reluctantly and turned it over and over in his hand.

"Open it, Jimmie," said Alma impatiently. "You can't keep the girl waiting."

A thin youth with a mop of red hair lurched forward, and before the messenger could divine his intention he had clipped her round the waist.

"She's the partner I've been waiting for," he said hilariously. "Start up the old piano, Billy!"

The girl struggled to escape but found herself pushed and swayed to the tune that was hammered forth from the piano-player and saw nothing in the vacuous faces about her but grinning approval.

"Let me go!" she cried. "Please let me go. You ought not to – "

"Dance, old darling, dance!" hiccoughed the youth, and then suddenly he felt a hand upon his wrist.

"Let that lady go, please, Molton." It was Augustus Javot.

"You mind your own damn business," said the angry young man, but with a smile Javot gently disengaged the girl.

"I'm sorry," he murmured, and took no further notice of her captor.

James Tynewood was opening the letter and Javot was too intent upon watching his face to interest himself in the muttered threats at his elbow. He saw Tynewood blink drunkenly at the letter and read word by word the brief communication, and then suddenly the colour left the face of the baronet and his lower lip trembled.

"What is the matter?" asked Alma sharply, for she too had observed the signs.

Slowly the young man crushed the letter in his hands and a look of malignity came to his face.

"Curse him, he has come back!" he said thickly.

"Who has come back?"

He did not reply for a moment and then: "The man I hate of all men in the world!" he said, thrusting the letter into his pocket.

He turned his eyes upon the girl.

"Is there any message?" she asked timidly. She was still white and shaking.

"You can tell Vance that he can go to hell," said Sir James Tynewood. "Give me some brandy, somebody!"

THE MAN FROM PRETORIA

Marjorie Stedman, confidential stenographer to the firm of Vance & Vance, left Park Buildings, happy to find herself again in the cool air of a spring evening. So that was Sir James Tynewood! Hitherto he had been a name written upon one of the black deed boxes in her employer's office.

Sir James Tynewood! The bearer of an ancient and honoured name, a name which to her mind recalled the chivalry of ancient days – and he was a drunkard, a sot, a vulgarian who consorted with that kind of company!

She shivered at the recollection.

She reached the office in Bloomsbury after all the clerks had left. Mr Vance, grey-haired, was waiting for her in his own office and he looked at her curiously as she entered.

"Well, Miss Stedman, did you deliver my letter?" he asked.

"Yes, Mr Vance," she said.

"To Sir James Tynewood?"

She nodded. The lawyer was eyeing her more keenly.

"What is the matter with you? You look a little pale. Have you had an accident?"

She shook her head.

"I had rather an uncomfortable experience," she said, and related what had happened.

The lawyer bit his lip in annoyance.

"I am sorry. I did not think you would be subjected to that kind of treatment or I would have gone myself," he said. "You quite understand, Miss Stedman, that I could not send one of the clerks."

7

"I know the message was confidential," she acknowledged. She did not tell him that she had wondered why a clerk had not taken that letter, and as if reading her thoughts the lawyer said:

"One day you will know why I asked you to go to see – Sir James Tynewood," he said. "I am very much obliged to you indeed. I suppose Sir James gave you no answer?"

She hesitated.

"He gave me one which I shouldn't care to repeat, for it was somewhat uncomplimentary to you, Mr Vance," she said with a smile.

The lawyer nodded.

"It is a bad business," he said after a pause. "You're sure Sir James said nothing else?"

"Not to me," replied the girl. "He said – " she hesitated again. "A lady asked him what the message was about and he replied that the man he hated had come back."

"The man he hated!" repeated the lawyer with a sad little smile.

Then with a shrug of his shoulders he rose.

"It's a bad business," he repeated as he reached for his coat from the hook on the wall, and then as though changing the subject – "so we're losing you at the end of the week, Miss Stedman?"

"Yes, Mr Vance, I'm sorry to go. I've been very happy here."

"From a selfish point of view, I'm sorry too," said the lawyer, struggling into his coat; "but for your sake I am very pleased. Has your uncle found that gold reef he was looking for?"

The girl smiled.

"No, but he has made a lot of money in South Africa, and he's been awfully good to mother and myself. You did not know Uncle Solomon, did you?"

"I met him once twenty years ago," said the lawyer. "Your father brought him to the office one day and he struck me as being rather a character."

He walked to the door and stood as though waiting for her to pass out.

"You've no more work to do?" he said in surprise, as she showed no intention of following him.

The girl smiled.

"I have the statement of claim for James Vesson to type before I go," she said, and Mr Vance uttered an exclamation of impatience.

"What a fool I am! Why of course," he said. "I ought not to have sent you out. But won't it do in the morning, Miss Stedman?" he asked half-heartedly, for he knew that the statement had to be filed early.

She shook her head laughingly.

"I really don't mind staying a little late, Mr Vance," she replied. "I have nothing to do tonight, and the statement will only take me two hours, and I would much rather do it tonight than come up early in the morning."

"Very well," said Mr Vance. "Good night, Miss Stedman. I have only just time to catch my train to Brighton. I will ring you up in the morning and you can tell me if there is any news of importance."

Left alone, she passed into the little room leading out of the lawyer's office, and in a few minutes her typewriter was clattering rapidly as she made an attempt to overtake her arrears of work.

She had reached the fourth folio of a long, dry and monotonous statement of claim, when she thought she heard a knock at the door of the outer office and paused, listening. The knock was repeated and she rose, wondering what belated client had appeared at this late hour of the evening.

She opened the door, expecting to find a telegraph boy, but to her surprise the figure of a man confronted her. He was a tall man, dressed in a shabby grey flannel suit, and she noted in that odd, inconsequential way which people have when taking their first impression of a stranger, that he wore no collar or tie. A soft white shirt, open at the neck, a battered grey Stetson hat on the back of his head, completed the mental picture. His lean, good-looking face was tanned to a dull mahogany, and a pair of grey, watchful eyes surveyed her.

"Is Mr Vance in?" he asked curtly, though she noticed he took off his hat when he spoke to her.

"No, Mr Vance has been gone ten minutes," said the girl.

The stranger licked his lips.

"Do you know where I can find him?" he asked.

She shook her head.

"Ordinarily, I could tell you," she said with a smile, "though it isn't customary to give Mr Vance's private address to visitors. But tonight he has gone to Brighton to stay with a friend over the weekend, and he did not leave his address." She hesitated. "Perhaps you would like to give me your name?" she asked and he hesitated.

"Are you likely to get into communication with him?"

She nodded.

"He will call me on the 'phone tomorrow morning to discover if there is anything which requires his attention," she said. "I could give him your name then."

He still stood in the passage and realizing that this man, in spite of his unprepossessing attire, might be some client of importance, she pulled the door wider open.

"Won't you come and sit down for a moment?" she said. "Perhaps you would like to write a message to Mr Vance?"

He came slowly into the room and stood for a moment looking at the chair she had drawn forward for him.

"No, I won't write anything," he said after a pause. "But when he calls up tomorrow, will you tell him that Mr Smith has arrived from Pretoria?"

He spoke deliberately and emphatically.

"You will remember – Mr Smith from Pretoria. And tell him I want him to get into communication with me at once."

"Mr Smith from Pretoria," she repeated, scribbling down the name on a scrap of paper, and wondering how important this Pretoria Smith might be.

She had a vague feeling that, although he was looking at her steadily, he was not seeing her. A little frown upon his forehead spoke eloquently of his preoccupation, and she had the sensation of being looked through, rather than being looked at.

He stared down at the desk again.

"I will write a message," he said. "Can you give me pen and paper?"

"There is pen and paper on the table," she laughed in spite of herself, and a dull-red flush came into the tanned face.

"I am very sorry," he stammered apologetically, "but I am not seeing things today."

"I had that impression too," said the girl, and a faint smile showed at the corner of the man's mouth.

She went to the farther end of the room for fear he thought she might be overlooking him as he wrote; but he seemed to find some difficulty in framing the words he had to put upon the paper. He sat for fully five minutes, nibbling the end of his pen.

"No, I won't write," he said, and put the pen down as he got up to his feet. "Just tell Mr Vance that Mr Smith of Pretoria called. I think that will be sufficient. He knows where to find me."

There was a footstep in the corridor outside, the handle of the door turned and it opened. The newcomer was evidently in too much hurry to knock.

"Where's Vance?" he asked as he came in. It was Sir James Tynewood, a little dishevelled and red of face.

"Mr Vance has gone," said the girl, but Sir James made no reply. He was staring at the shabby man from Pretoria.

"My God!" he said in a quaking voice. "You – Jot!"

They stood looking at each other, the half-drunken young baronet and the man from Pretoria, and the latter's face was fixed in an inscrutable mask. The silence which followed was painful for the girl. She sensed a tragedy here, and her quick intuitions placed her in a moment upon the side of the South African visitor.

"Do you know Sir James Tynewood?" she faltered.

Slowly the head of Pretoria Smith turned towards her, and he showed his white teeth in a mirthless smile.

"I know Sir James Tynewood very well," he said, and then addressing the other, he said sternly: "You will meet me tomorrow evening at the Chase, Sir James Tynewood."

The young man stood shaking in every limb, his face a sickly white, his head bent.

"I will see you tomorrow," he mumbled huskily and staggered from the room.

THE SURPRISING DEBTS

"I am sure something has upset you, dear. You've never been so snappy with me before," complained Mrs Stedman.

Her whole attitude toward life was one of complaint, and the girl was inured to this form of persecution. They sat at breakfast in a tiny Brixton flat, and Mrs Stedman, who, in spite of her frequent predictions of an early demise, had managed to eat a very hearty breakfast, was sitting watching her daughter over her glasses with a disapproving frown.

"There is nothing the matter with me, mother," said Marjorie Stedman quietly. "I had rather an upsetting day at the office yesterday. Something extraordinary happened."

"And you won't tell your own mother what it is!" repeated Mrs Stedman for the third time.

"Don't you understand, mother," said the girl patiently, "that the business of my employer is, or should be, sacred, and that I cannot talk about it?"

"Not even to your own mother?" murmured Mrs Stedman, shaking her head. "Marjorie, I have always given you the greatest confidence, and I have repeatedly asked you to come to me with all your troubles."

"Well, this isn't one of my troubles really," smiled the girl. "It is somebody else's trouble which does not concern me and should not concern you, mother dear."

Mrs Stedman sighed heavily.

"I shall be very glad when you're away from that wretched office," she said. "It is not good for a young girl to be mixed up in crimes and divorces and all those terrible things one reads about in the Sunday papers."

Marjorie rested her hand on her mother's shoulder as she walked past her.

"Mother dear, I've told you often that Mr Vance has nothing to do with crime," she said. "We haven't had a criminal in our office for a hundred years."

"Don't say 'our office,' my dear," wailed Mrs Stedman. "It sounds so low! And please, when we get into the country, amongst people of our own class, never talk about your business. If people knew that you were connected with trade – "

"Oh, mother, what nonsense you talk!" said the girl, losing patience at last. "Just because Uncle Solomon is sending us enough money to live comfortably in the country, you don't suppose we're going to put on airs or meet people who will be shocked by my being a typist in a lawyer's office?"

"Confidential secretary," corrected Mrs Stedman firmly. "I insist upon your being a confidential secretary. I cannot allow you to call yourself a typist, my dear. I've told all my friends that you're studying for the Bar."

The girl groaned.

"Oh Heavens!" she said.

"It isn't what we shall be next month," Mrs Stedman went on with satisfaction. "In a year's time, when your uncle gets rich, we are going to take the beautiful house in which I was born, my dear – the country estate of the Stedmans."

The country estate of the Stedmans consisted of three and a half acres of excellent paddock and garden, and Marjorie had once made a pilgrimage to Tynewood –

Tynewood! Why, that must be Sir James Tynewood's estate. She wondered if it was so, and resolved to ask Mr Vance at the earliest opportunity.

On her way to town that morning she went over the events of the previous night. What hold had this stranger from the South over Sir James Tynewood, she wondered? She would never forget the white face of the baronet when he had caught sight of the man in shabby grey. There was terror in one face and condemnation in the other. Was it blackmail? Was it the knowledge of some indiscretion of Sir James which gave this strange man power over the other?

She found it hard to accept this view. There was something in Pretoria Smith's face which precluded the possibility of such an explanation. If ever honesty and steadfast purpose shone in a man's eyes, they showed in Pretoria Smith's.

She reached the office half an hour earlier than was usual. She did not wish to miss Mr Vance's telephone call, which came to her at eleven o'clock.

"Is everything all right, Miss Stedman?" he asked, and then she told him of the visitor.

"Smith?" said his voice sharply. "From Pretoria? I didn't expect him for a week. I am coming up to town straight away."

"He left no address," said the girl.

"I know where to find him," said Mr Vance. "Did he say anything?"

"Nothing at all," said the girl, "beyond what I have told you. Sir James came whilst he was here."

She heard his exclamation.

"They met in the office? What happened?" asked the lawyer's voice anxiously.

"Nothing happened except that Sir James looked awfully worried and ill and went out immediately."

There was a long pause, and she thought he had hung up the telephone receiver. Presently he said:

"I am coming up by the eleven-forty-five. I shall be at the office just before one. Get your lunch early. Have you seen the newspapers?" he asked.

"No," she said in surprise. It was an unusual inquiry from him. "What has happened?

"Nothing, except that Sir James Tynewood is married to Alma Trebizond, the actress," said the lawyer grimly. "There is going to be some bad trouble in the Tynewood family."

Surprise was to follow surprise for the girl that day. In the course of the morning came another stranger to the office – a stout, cheerful man, evidently of Hebraic origin. It was the practice of the firm to refer new business to the managing clerk; but he also was on a holiday and the visitor was shown into the girl.

"I understand you're Mr Vance's confidential secretary?" he said. "Is it possible to see Mr Vance today?"

She shook her head.

"Mr Vance is coming to town on very important business, but I do not think that he wants to attend to any other," she said. "Is there anything I can do for you?"

The man put his silk hat carefully on the table and took out a large pocket-book and extracted a document.

"Well, miss, there's no secret about this," he said. "I've got to see Mr Vance some time before Monday, and if I can't see him I'd like you to tell him that Mr Hawkes, of Hawkes & Ferguson, financiers, called with reference to Sir James Tynewood's debts."

"Sir James Tynewood's debts?" she repeated, puzzled, and he nodded.

"The young gentleman owes me twenty-five thousand pounds, borrowed on note of hand, and I'm getting a bit rattled about it. He keeps on renewing his bills and borrowing a bit more, and I want to see Mr Vance before I make any further advances."

"But Sir James Tynewood is a very rich man," said the girl.

"And I'm a very poor man," said the other with a grin, "and I want a bit of my stuff back."

"Have you already seen Mr Vance?"

The visitor shook his head.

"No. Sir James has asked me to keep away from his lawyers, but matters have gone a little bit too far for me, miss. I'm a business man, and I have no respect for titles, being a democrat. The only titles that interest me are titles of property. I've kept away from Vance & Vance as long as I could, but I must have a bit on account. You see, miss, I'm a moneylender," he went on confidentially, "and moneylenders know one another's business. I happen to know that Sir James has borrowed a lot of money from Crewe & Jacobsen and from Bedsons Ltd., and half a dozen other firms; and what's more, he's been going the pace in the West End. He's in debt left and right – why, he owes the motor-car people in Bond Street over three thousand pounds for that car he gave to Alma Trebizond. When I saw the announcement in the paper this morning that he'd got married, I said to myself: 'Well, now, this is the time for me to have a bit of a marriage settlement!' "

He chuckled at his feeble jest. Then, lowering his voice:

"Now, look here, miss, I'm a business man and you're a business woman. I'll tell you frankly, I have got scared about this money, and if you can put in a word to Vance so that my claim's settled first, why, there's a handsome commission for you."

"I'm afraid I'm not in the habit of taking commissions," said the girl coldly, "and I'm not even in a position to accept your confidence. I am merely Mr Vance's confidential stenographer, and I'm not so sure that he will be very pleased to hear that you have confided in me."

That ended the interview and Marjorie Stedman's acquaintance with the firm of Hawkes & Ferguson. When Vance arrived she told him of the conversation and he was unusually grave.

"Moneylenders, eh?" he said quietly. "I suspected something of that sort. Telegraph to Mr Herman to come into the office."

Mr Herman was his managing clerk.

"I won't bother you with this business, but Herman must go round and see these moneylenders and find out how much money this foolish boy owes."

"But Mr Vance, isn't Sir James very rich?"

"Very," said Mr Vance dryly.

That afternoon, although it was Saturday, there were many comings and goings at the office. Mr Herman arrived and apparently went round in a taxicab interviewing Sir James Tynewood's creditors, or as many as could be found at that inconvenient period of the week.

WHAT HAPPENED
AT TYNEWOOD CHASE

At Vance's suggestion she had stayed on until late in the afternoon. There was no work for her to do, but she supposed that sooner or later her services would be requisitioned, and in this surmise she was right. At five o'clock her bell rang and she went into Mr Vance's office. He was sealing a large envelope which evidently contained the results of his work that afternoon, for he had spent his time writing. He had sealed the flap and was dipping his pen into the ink preparatory to writing the address, when he paused irresolutely.

"H'm!" he said. "That is awkward."

Then he wrote the name.

"Sir James Tynewood, Bart.," she read over his shoulder, with a sense of dismay, because she guessed that she was to be the bearer of this letter, and she had not forgotten her experience of the previous night.

Then, to her surprise, he took from his stationery rack a still larger envelope and put the first within, sealing it again. This time he wrote a name which was strange to her – "Dr Fordham, Tynewood Chase, Tynewood."

He sat for a moment deep in thought and then raised his spectacled face to hers with a little smile.

"Miss Stedman," he said, "I want you to take a journey into the country. Do you know Tynewood?"

She nodded.

"It is in Droitshire," he explained. "You can get a train from Paddington at five-forty-five, and you should be there before eight. The nearest station is about three miles from Tynewood Chase, but I will telegraph to the *Red Lion Inn* to have a fly – I suppose that up-to-date establishment has motorcars for hire now," he smiled. "At any rate, you'll have no difficulty in getting to the Chase, and you should be back in town at eleven o'clock tonight. There is a good train leaving the Junction at nine. You understand, you are to place this letter in the hands of Dr Fordham."

She nodded.

"There is one more thing I want to say, Miss Stedman," said Vance, a little uneasily. "Since you have been my confidential secretary you have heard a great many ugly secrets which I am sure are safe with you. But the secret of Sir James Tynewood is uglier than any," he said. "I can only hope," he added, "that you will not make any discovery without my assistance. But if you do, Miss Stedman, I ask you to treat all you see and hear tonight, and all you saw and heard when I entrusted you with the previous commission, as a secret inviolable and unbetrayable."

"Of course, Mr Vance," she said. "But – " she hesitated.

"But what?" he asked sharply.

"Oh, it's nothing to do with the business," she said. "I wondered whether I could get a message to mother telling her that I shall not be home until late. She expected me at two o'clock."

"I'll send a messenger boy – or why not telegraph?"

The girl laughed.

"A telegram always worries mother," she said. She did not explain that the doleful Mrs Stedman was of such a sanguine temperament that she expected miracles at every rat-tat of the door, and was correspondingly depressed when the message which came brought no roseate news.

The journey to Dilmot Junction seemed unending, though she had provided herself with a book and papers, and she stepped out on the rain-drenched platform at Dilmot relieved to find her journey over.

Mr Vance had evidently telegraphed, for an ancient and wheezy motor car was waiting for her.

Happily it was a closed car, for heavy rain was falling. As the antiquated machine rattled and coughed through the dark lanes, it occurred to the girl that it was within a few miles of this place that she would be living in a month's time. Despite the unwillingness of the old car to ascend hills, and the alarming rapidity with which it descended them, it made a good steady progress, and presently it bumped through the main street of a village. She looked through the rain-splashed windows, noted half a dozen shops, and then the car ran into the darkness again.

"That must be Tynewood," she thought, and in this she was correct.

Presently the car stopped, and, lowering the window, she saw tall iron gates to which, in response to the furious summons of the cabman's motor-horn, came a dark figure in a mackintosh.

"Who is there?" it shouted. "I can't let you into the Park."

The girl leant out of the window.

"I am from Mr Vance the lawyer, and I have an important letter for Dr Fordham," she said.

Without further parley the gate was opened and the car sped up a long, winding drive, flanked on either side by tall trees, and presently stopped again.

The girl looked out. The big house was in darkness, and the only light came through a semicircular transom above the wide doorway at which they had stopped. She got out of the cab, bidding the man wait, and had to requisition one of the car's lights to discover the old-fashioned bell-pull. The clang of the bell came faintly, but it was a long time before anybody answered. Then she heard quick steps within the stone-flagged hall, there was a rattle of chains, a click of a lock, and the door opened a foot.

The man who stood there was a stranger to her.

"Who is it?" he asked brusquely.

"I'm from Mr Vance," said Marjorie Stedman. "I have an important letter for Dr Fordham."

"I am he," said the man. "Will you come in?"

He closed the door behind her and took the letter from her hand.

"Sit down for a moment, please," he said, and she found a seat on one of the big oaken chairs which stood on either side of the hall.

"This is for Sir James," he said as he opened the first envelope. "Just one moment."

He was halfway up the hall when he turned back.

"You don't mind waiting here? It is not very comfortable, but I'm sorry I can't for the moment do any better for you. I hope you have had your dinner, because there is nobody here to give you food. None of the servants are in the house."

Marjorie had not had dinner and was beginning to feel the need for that meal, but smilingly she shook her head.

"It doesn't matter at all; I'm not hungry," she said untruthfully.

"You won't move from here?" he asked again.

"Of course not," said the girl, a little piqued. "I can go back to the Junction now, can't I? I have a cab outside."

"Wait a moment," said Dr Fordham, and hurried along the hall and into a room which led from it.

He closed the door behind him, but apparently the lock did not catch. From where she sat she could see the door opening slowly, and there came to her distinctly the sound of voices.

"I'm ruined anyway," said one bitterly, and she knew it was Sir James Tynewood who was speaking. "Oh, my God, what a fool I have been, what a fool!"

"You've a chance to get right," said another voice, and the voice seemed familiar. "I've given you a chance, and you're a fool if you don't take it."

"How can I?" almost screamed the voice of Sir James. "Do you think I can go to London and face that crowd? Do you think I can tell them – "

There was a muttered interruption, evidently that of the doctor. She heard the tearing of the envelope she had brought and the rustle of papers. Silence followed, broken only by the crackle of the leaves as they were turned; and then a voice:

"You madman, you madman!" it said.

There was no reply for a second.

"What is it?" asked Sir James in a low voice and there was another silence.

She guessed that the letter had been handed to the other, for no word was spoken for fully two minutes. Then it was the drawling voice she heard:

"I'm going to settle with you – "

There was the deafening report of a shot, and the girl sprang to her feet, white as death. A silence; then the voice said: "My God! I've killed him!"

She ran to the door and pushed it open. Sir James Tynewood lay upon the floor in a pool of blood and a man was leaning over him, holding a revolver in his hand. At the sound of the opening door he sprang to his feet – it was Pretoria Smith!

THE MYSTERY

Another second, and Fordham had rushed her from the room, gripping the girl by the arm, and half led, half dragged her to the door.

"You've got a cab here, haven't you?" he said. "A motor-cab?"

"What – what is wrong?" she stammered.

He made no reply, but, opening the door, he pushed her into the stormy night, following and closing the door behind him. He gave some direction to the cabman which she could not overhear.

"Get in," he said impatiently.

"What has happened?" she asked again. "Are you going for the police?"

He did not reply to this inquiry either. They went through the village again and stopped at the farthermost end, and only then did he speak.

"Young lady," he said, "you must go back to Mr Vance, and until you see him you are not to speak of what you have seen to a living soul. Do you understand that?"

The girl was bewildered, half-hysterical, and her lips trembled as she replied.

"N-no."

"I will get Mr Vance on the 'phone. He will be at his office, he said so in his letter."

"Is Sir James dead?"

"I hope not," said the doctor briefly, and with these words left her.

She was surprised to find Mr Vance waiting on the platform when the train drew in to Paddington. Occupied as she was with her thoughts, the journey had passed in an amazingly short time, and it was not till she reached London that she realized how famished she was.

"You haven't had any dinner, the doctor tells me," said Mr Vance. "I am taking you straight away to eat, and then after I can talk to you."

"You have heard from Dr Fordham?"

He nodded.

"Is – is Sir James – ?"

"Now, you're not to ask questions until you have fed," said Vance with an attempt at good humour which he was far from feeling. "I am taking you to my house in Grosvenor Place."

It was not until she had finished her meal at his earnest solicitation, and had choked down half a glassful of port, that he referred to Sir James Tynewood and the tragedy which had overtaken him.

"Now, in the first place, let me reassure you on one matter. Sir James Tynewood is not dead."

"Thank God for that!" said the girl with a sigh of relief. "I was so awfully afraid – "

"It was just a superficial wound and he has quite recovered. In fact," said the lawyer, speaking deliberately and emphatically, "he is well enough to leave for abroad tomorrow."

The girl stared at him.

"Is Sir James going abroad?"

He nodded.

"Is his wife, Lady Tynewood, going also?"

"His wife is not going," said Vance.

"But I – I don't understand."

"There's a great deal that you won't understand for many years about this matter," said Mr Vance. "But I want you to believe me. He is leaving by the mailboat *Carisbrooke Castle* tomorrow afternoon."

She shook her head hopelessly.

"I'm afraid I'm not good at solving mysteries," she said and then asked: "Where is Mr Smith of Pretoria? Is he going too?"

The lawyer took his cigar from his teeth and regarded it critically.

"Mr Smith of Pretoria accompanies Sir James," he said slowly. "And now I'm going to send you home in my car."

If Marjorie Stedman had been in an uncommunicative mood in the morning, she was sphinx-like that night, and the baffled Mrs Stedman, curious to know what had kept her daughter so late and what had thrown her into this unusually agitated mood, gave up her inquiries in exasperation.

The mystery of the events at Tynewood Chase were to deepen for the girl. She reported for duty on Monday morning as usual, and found Mr Vance apparently oblivious to all that had happened on the Saturday. After the part she had played in this strange Tynewood drama, she found the routine of the office dull and uninteresting. She did not see much of the lawyer. He had a bell-push on his table, and only summoned her when he required her. Owing to the peculiar nature of the business in which be was engaged, it was understood that he was not to be interrupted and any inquiry that had to be put through to him, or any question which had to be settled, had to be made by telephone after a preliminary inquiry by telephone whether he was disengaged.

But Mr Vance had an absent-minded trick of pressing the bell when the girl was not required. It happened almost every day that his idle fingers would rest abstractedly on the bell-push and the girl would answer the summons to discover that she was not required. Late on the Monday afternoon, as she was preparing to go, the bell rang shrilly and she gathered up her notebook and pencil and opened the door communicating with Vance's office.

A man was sitting on the opposite side of the table and she recognized him immediately as Dr Fordham, and stopped dead, guessing that the bell had been rung by her employer in one of his moments of aberration. Neither Dr Fordham nor Vance saw her, for they were deeply intent upon the matter they were discussing, and she was backing out when Vance spoke.

"So he is dead," he said. "Poor boy, poor boy!"

"Quite dead," said Fordham. "I thought I told you on the 'phone that there was no possible hope of his recovery."

She stepped back into her room quickly and closed the door softly behind her and stood with her hand resting on the handle.

Dead! Sir James Tynewood was dead! Why had the lawyer lied? And whose hand had struck down the husband of Alma Trebizond?

IN SOUTH AFRICA

There was a discussion at the waterhole on the edge of the Kalahari Desert. It was between Wilhelm the Fingo and Jan the half-breed bushman, and it concerned one Solomon Stedman who lay with blue lips, gasping out his life, within sight of the water that would have saved it.

The discussion was conducted in the *taal*, which is Dutch as it is spoken by half-breed kitchen-maids and farm-workers.

"I think the *baas* will die at sundown," said Wilhelm, "and then we can take his curious instruments to the resident magistrate at Vrykloof, keeping his money for ourselves. The little mine he has found we can own and we shall be rich. Then I shall go back to T'simo and buy cattle and wives."

"You are a fool," retorted the dispassionate Jan, "for native people are not allowed to own mines in this land. We will let him die and take his money."

All this old Solomon heard and his glazing eyes turned malignantly upon his unfaithful servants.

"I am no fool," said the Fingo man, "for I am a Christian and can write my name. And I know a poor white man in Mafekin' who will make the claim for me. He lives with a Matabele woman whom I have known."

Into this debate intruded Pretoria Smith. He knew the location of the waterhole, having prospected this country before. He had a week's growth of beard, but he had been tired of life for six months. The sands of the desert were in his throat and he humped a pack, which was heavy but not quite as heavy as his heart, for his nights were full of dreams, dreams of a dead boy lying at his feet in the big hall at Tynewood Chase.

At his belt, in a two-inch holster, hung a long and dangerous weapon, the barrel of which was polished bright in places.

He stood for a second looking at the group, then his eyes fell upon the dying man.

"Do you let the *baas* lie there when he is parching for water?" he demanded hoarsely – you get hoarse in a ten-mile trek through a land which is mainly salt sand and *wacht ein bitje* bushes.

Jan was a half-breed, and therefore a coward. Wilhelm was of the Fingo people and in consequence was born with the soul of a slave. They both foresaw desperate developments and strove to avert the coming trouble.

"*Baas*," said Wilhelm, "this man has found a good little reef which shows gold in the rock so that you can pick it out with the point of a knife. If he dies we will be all – "

The revolver jerked out and with a squeal in chorus the men ducked and lifted Solomon Stedman and laid him beside the water, turning him over so that his dry lips could suck the wonder-fluid.

It was two hours before Solomon Stedman could find the voice and energy to talk, and then he employed the first few minutes of recovered speech in cursing all half-breed bushmen, Kaffirs and other aborigines of South Africa.

Pretoria Smith, who had started a fire and was slicing biltong into a small cooking-pot, laughed softly.

"If it hadn't been for you, lad," said the old man, "I should have been a dead 'un, and the Stedman reef would have been staked by some other prospector – you ain't a prospector, are you?" he asked suspiciously.

"We're all prospectors," said Pretoria Smith easily. "If you mean, am I prospecting for gold, I can relieve your mind. I am not."

The old man was looking at him keenly.

"No, you ain't a prospector; you're a gentleman, ain't you?" he asked. "But you're not a new chum, I'll swear."

"Not exactly," replied the other, cutting off the top of a tin of vegetables and emptying the contents into the pot. "I've shot up and down this country since I was a boy of seventeen. In fact, when I left Eton."

Pretoria Smith was not usually so communicative, but the old man had a trick of drawing confidences.

"I was in German West Africa and German East Africa during the war," Smith went on. "In fact, I've not spent six months at a time away from this infernal continent since I was a kid."

"Where are you going now?" asked the other.

Pretoria Smith shrugged his shoulders.

"Anywhere for a change," he said vaguely.

The old man was very thoughtful through the meal which followed, and sat by the fire pulling at his pipe, staring hard into the dancing flames. Presently he knocked the ashes out of his pipe deliberately and asked:

"Do you want to make your fortune?"

Pretoria Smith, deep in his own thoughts, looked up sharply.

"What do you mean?" he asked.

"Well," said the old man slowly, "I have found the Kalahari reef."

"The devil you have!" said Pretoria Smith. "I thought that was one of the legends of Africa. People have always thought there was a reef in the Kalahari Desert, but it's never been found."

"I've found it," said Solomon Stedman triumphantly. "Now, what do you say?"

"To what?"

"To coming in with me. I want a younger man, and I owe you something for what you did today."

"Don't be a fool," said Pretoria Smith pleasantly. "Who wouldn't give a dying man water? I want no decorations for that. And I want no fortunes either. I've quite enough to get along with."

Solomon Stedman stared at him.

"You're the first lad I've ever met that didn't want money," he chuckled. "Well, it's not going to be so easy to get, or perhaps I shouldn't offer you a share. The reef's got to be proved and prospected, and it means a year's hard work. Then I'll have to get the money to float the mine, and that'll want some doing."

Pretoria Smith scratched his unshaven chin.

"Work attracts me more than the wealth," he smiled, and Solomon took that as an acceptance of his offer.

He spoke about his own life and his struggles after a while, though Pretoria Smith volunteered no further information about himself.

"Mind you," said the old man, "even if I make good on this reef, I've neither kith nor kin to leave my money to. There's a kid in England, the daughter of my brother – he was a bit of a fool, was Fred – and she's the only relation I have in the world. Minnie, her name is – no, Margaret – no – " He fumbled in his pocket and produced a bundle of letters from which he extracted one. "Marjorie, that's the name," he said, setting a pair of old pince-nez on his nose. "Marjorie. A regular girl she is. She's written me since she was a baby."

"Indeed!" said Pretoria Smith politely. He was not particularly interested in the relatives of Solomon Stedman, and found more pleasure in watching the incongruous picture of this rough man with the glasses set askew on his nose.

"A well-educated young lady, she is," nodded Solomon Stedman. "My brother Fred was well educated too, though he didn't know enough to get out of the rain and was always spending about ten per cent more than he earned. Have you ever heard of the Stedmans in England?"

"I can't remember having met one," smiled Pretoria Smith. "But then, of course, I don't know many people in England, and very few people know me."

"I've been keeping his widow for years," boasted the old man complacently. "Just a few pounds a month to help things along, you understand. I've been able to send her more lately, and if we get the reef going, my boy – " He shook his head at the magnificence of the prospect.

Solomon Stedman had not exaggerated the difficulties or the arduous character of the undertaking. For six months under a blazing sun the two men trekked and prospected, dug big cuttings in the sandy soil, sampled quartz which often had to be carried twenty miles to the nearest water for washing; and in those six months Pretoria Smith managed to forget a lot of things he did not wish to remember. The reef was located and proved beyond doubt. Expert engineers came up from Johannesburg, mining officials arrived importantly from Cape Town; licences were assessed and paid; and twelve months after their meeting, the first four-stamp mill was thundering on the very spot where Solomon Stedman had made his recovery.

But in that time the friendship between the two men had grown in strength; and although Solomon, who prided himself upon his artfulness, had failed to discover anything further about his partner, the reticence of Pretoria Smith rather helped to tighten the bond between them than to loosen it. The friendship was measured by a year and the fractions of years. The four-stamp mill had multiplied itself, and the little township of Stedmanville had come into being. A huge pumping plant to bring the water, and the installation of an electric power house, had occupied Pretoria Smith's fullest attentions, and he began to share the pride of the old man in this great achievement.

Two years had passed when the old man met his younger partner at the head of the main shaft.

"Remember that sister-in-law of mine?" he asked. He had reached the age when he repeated stories over and over again, and Pretoria Smith had had little chance of forgetting the unfortunate lady whom old Solomon invariably described as "a useless kind of woman." "Well, it appears she's got a nephew she's sending out."

"Fine!" said Pretoria Smith. "Where is she sending him out from?"

"She's sending him out from England, of course," said Solomon. "He's arriving next week. According to my sister, there's a sort of engagement between this lad and Lily – Margaret – "

"Marjorie," suggested Pretoria Smith with a little grin. "What a forgetful old devil you are!"

"Ain't I?" said Solomon, lost in self-admiration. "Well, this young spark and my niece are mashed on one another."

"Solomon, Solomon," reproved Pretoria Smith, shaking his head, "you're a vulgar old man! And why shouldn't he be 'mashed' on her, anyway? It's the way of the young, Solomon. We old gentlemen do not understand such things."

"Old!" scoffed Solomon. "Why, you're only a kid yourself! His name," he went on, consulting a letter, "is Lance Kelman."

"And a very pretty name too," said Smith, slapping the other on the shoulder. "Now do you want me to meet the gentleman in the family Ford, or is he walking?"

Solomon apparently had ideas of his partner going to Kimberley to meet the visitor, but this suggestion Pretoria Smith vetoed, and was not sorry he took this stand when Mr Lance Kelman disgorged himself and some half a dozen large trunks from the Bulawayo mail one spring morning, and stood gazing disconsolately around the unpromising landscape.

He was a beautifully tailored young man, wearing the kit which he regarded as being appropriate to travel in the wilds. His tight-kneed, baggy breeches were of exquisite cut, his white shirt was silk and stainless, and he wore a coat shaped at the waist. The only person in sight on the platform when he arrived was Pretoria Smith, who watched the accumulation of luggage with a feeling of wonder and awe. Presently Mr Lance Kelman, looking round, caught sight of the tall figure and beckoned him.

"I say," he said loudly, "how can I get to Mr Solomon Stedman's mine? I am his nephew."

"You can reach the mine on my humble motor car," said Pretoria Smith, "and I will send an ox-waggon for your baggage."

"Oh, you've come to meet me, have you?" said Mr Lance Kelman patronizingly. "Well, you might tell these fellows what to do with the baggage until your waggon comes. I shall want to take some things with me, of course."

"There will be room for your vanity bag," said Pretoria Smith good-humouredly as he picked up a polished dressing-case and led the way to the car. "You'll get the rest of your stuff by the evening."

The newcomer looked at him suspiciously. "I'm Mr Solomon Stedman's nephew," he said again with emphasis.

"So you remarked before," replied Pretoria Smith coolly. "Does that mean you'd rather come by the ox-waggon?"

"Now, don't be insolent, my friend," said Lance Kelman loudly and Smith chuckled.

The journey back to the mine was completed in dignified silence as far as Lance Kelman was concerned. Even when he was introduced to Pretoria Smith as the partner of the old man, his attitude did not unbend.

"Well, what do you think of my nephew?" asked Solomon when the young man had been taken to the galvanized-iron hut which was to be his home during his stay.

"He's very pretty," answered Pretoria Smith cautiously. "So that's the young man your niece is engaged to?"

"Well, I don't know about engaged," hesitated Solomon. "Do you like him?"

"Next to a bad attack of mumps, he's the most popular thing I've been brought into contact with," said Pretoria Smith.

SOLOMON'S PLAN

Of Mr Kelman's three months' stay it is not necessary to speak in detail. He spoke incessantly and superiorly of "the old country," its wonders and advantages over "this uncivilized hole," and the two men listened in grave silence.

"I must go to England one of these days," said Pretoria Smith soberly. "It sounds a very interesting place."

"Of course, you'd be a bit lost in England," said the patronizing Mr Kelman, "but if ever you do come, you must ask me to show you round."

"Do you know him, too?" asked Pretoria Smith in an awe-stricken voice, and Mr Lance Kelman was pardonably puzzled.

He spoke too of Marjorie with a calm, proprietorial air, which made Pretoria Smith want to take him by the scruff of the neck and kick him. He referred to her as "Marje" and "my little girl" in a way which would have made Marjorie Stedman's hair stand on end.

A month after his arrival he disclosed the object of his visit. He had hinted that his relationship with old man Solomon entitled him to some share in his prosperity, but the suggestion was received in stony silence. He was even prepared to be a highly paid official of the company, preferably representing its interests in London. Old Solomon did not contemplate the same preparation. Then, crowning horror of the visit, the youth developed a form of German measles, which demanded hothouse fruits and careful nursing. Pretoria Smith nursed him, and, in the absence of more delicate fruit, compromised with ripe bananas.

"Thank God he's gone!" said Solomon Stedman when Pretoria Smith brought his tiny motor car to the steps of the office after seeing the visitor off.

Pretoria Smith laughed long and quietly, but to Solomon Stedman it was no laughing matter; for a new problem had entered into his calculations, and for the next few months he was a silent and thoughtful man.

One bitterly cold day in May, which is wintertime in the bush veld, old Solomon sat in his frame office, hung about with blue prints and section maps. His shaggy brows were set lower than usual and his coarse finger and thumb were pinching his chin. The cause of this visible evidence of perplexity was the letter he was reading.

He put the letter down and scratched his head. Pretoria Smith lounged into the office at that moment. The stem of a polished briar was between his strong white teeth, and the only advertisement of his prosperity was the gold safety pin that fastened his soft collar.

" 'Lo, Smith – come in."

"I'm in," said the other laconically, and the old man growled.

"Well, stay in, dam' ye! I've had a letter from my niece."

"I still find it difficult to believe that you have respectable relations," said Pretoria Smith.

"She's the daughter of my young brother – he's been dead a few years and better off he is, I'm sure," said the old man philosophically. "And Margret, Minnie, Maggy – here, what's the name at the bottom of this?"

He handed the letter to his partner and without glancing at it Pretoria Smith said wearily:

"Marjorie," and gave the letter back.

"Well, Marjorie – of course it is Marjorie; she used to write me when she was a baby almost. Marjorie, yes, of course it's Marjorie."

"Well, I'll admit that," said the patient Pretoria Smith; "what about it?"

"She's my only relation in the world."

Old Solomon scratched his bristly cheek and opened his mouth to assist in the process.

35

"You remember that bright boy that came out here last year to find a gold mine?"

Pretoria nodded. He hadn't had time to forget the youth in question. His arrogance, his attitude of superiority to things colonial, his general puppishness had stamped him in Smith's memory. He ranked second to a cattle disease which had carried off ten transport oxen in one week.

"Well, what about the elegant Lance?" demanded Pretoria Smith. "For a man of your advanced years, you have a hell of a lot of superfluous breath."

"Well, that's him," and Mr Solomon Stedman winked. Pretoria Smith laughed helplessly and knocked the ashes out of his pipe.

"That's him, is it? May I repeat what about him?"

"You know that she's sweet on him," said old Solomon, "not from what she said, but from what a fool of a mother wrote – I allow her four thousand a year, Smith. There's a bit in Maud's last letter about him, 'brave fellow…dangers…terrible journey across the desert…' and that sort of stuff."

"He came up by the Bulawayo train de luxe and had strawberries for tea. I brought him from the station in the new limousine. But I admit," said Pretoria Smith, "that I didn't put him to bed. Anyway, it doesn't matter, he's home now."

Solomon had an idea, a wonderful idea – Pretoria Smith recognized the symptoms.

"Pretoria," he said suddenly, "you and me have been pretty good pals. I've never forgotten what you did for me that day at the water-hole."

"Rubbish," said the other; "if I hadn't done what I did, I should have been a murderer."

"We've been pals," continued Solomon, and Pretoria Smith realized that this fact was the foundation for whatever would follow. "You're rich and I'm rich, Pretoria. I've got another winter – two at most – to live if that Kimberley doctor ain't a liar, and he oughtn't to be considering the money I paid him to come up here, and I've been worrying about what's going to happen to my money when I'm dead."

"You wicked old devil," said the other, affectionately gripping the old man's shoulder. "You ought to be worrying about what would happen to you when you were dead!"

"I'm all right," said Solomon with appalling complacence, "I guess I'll get past. No, it's the money. I can leave it to you – I can leave it to the Kimberley Hospital – but I don't want to. You're worth the better part of a million pounds. Now, this is where I come to the important bit. Are you married?"

He had never asked such a question of his partner before and he quaked at Pretoria's frown.

"No," said the man. "I'm not keen on women and never have been. I've been waiting to tell you for a long time, Solly, that my name isn't Smith."

"It's such an uncommon one that I thought it might be," said Solomon, "and I suppose you lived in Pretoria for a time?"

The other nodded.

"Well, what's your proposition?" he asked.

Mr Stedman chewed a large mint candy he had taken from a box and stared stonily out of the window.

"Go home and marry Marjorie," he said, and there was a dead silence in the little office. Then:

"You match-making old son of a gun!" said Pretoria admiringly, "and what do I do with Lance, smother him?"

"Lance!"

There was such scorn in old Solomon's voice that Pretoria chuckled.

"Yet another point," said Pretoria Smith, who was not averse to discussing the matter, since it possessed the element of novelty and charm. "What about Marjorie?"

Stedman of Stedman's Reef helped himself to another mint before he replied.

"Marjorie will be all right," he evaded. "She'll do anything to oblige me. I'm writing her."

37

Pretoria Smith had seated himself on the draughtsman's high stool and was gazing sombrely down upon the old man.

"I was afraid it might be for my good looks, my youth and other attractive qualities," he said dryly.

"You ain't bad," protested the other.

"Too old to call you uncle," said Pretoria with decision.

"You ain't over thirty – not much over. Don't get troublesome, Pretoria. I want it – that's all. I've got a feeling in my mind that this is the things that I've made my money for. It's worth making if you can get the grand sensation of having what you've tried for. As it is, I'd go out of the world feeling like a half-circle."

"But, Solly," pleaded the junior partner, "you don't seriously mean all this? Why, the girl would laugh at the idea. I don't care three fingers of rum whether I marry or not. I'd give her the run of the farm and the woods beyond and I'd never bother her."

"That ain't my idea." Solomon turned his eyes on the other and his shaggy brows were bent. "You've got to carry on my – race. That's the word. You've got to have children."

"Solomon, you're too thorough for me," said Pretoria Smith, "and now let us discuss No. 3 shaft which has gone punk, as I thought – "

"Damn No. 3 shaft – and No. 1, 2, 5 and 6," said Solomon impartially. "Keep to this idea of mine. Will you go back home and will you see Marjorie and put the question to her? If she says 'No,' well, you've done your share, Smith. I can't let her marry a 'dossie' like that pup of a boy."

Pretoria filled his pipe again, lit it and sat for some time fingering the fine hair of his shaggy yellow beard.

"All right," he said resigned, "but I wish your mind had been set on building an Orphans' Home."

"You'll save her from Lance," said Solomon. "That's one thing I forgot."

"It's almost worth the trip," answered Pretoria. "Besides, I may be saving Lance from her."

"She's my niece!" snorted Solomon.

"That's what I mean," nodded the other man. "By the way" – he was strolling out of the office – "where does your incomparable niece live?"

"At Tynewood."

"Great God!" said Pretoria Smith, and went white.

He sat down on the nearest chair and Solomon eyed him anxiously.

"You gave your word, Pretoria," he quavered, and the other man nodded.

After all, Tynewood did not know Pretoria Smith.

THE ORDER TO MARRY

I am an old man and have lived a hard life and the end may come at any moment. I cannot leave my hard-won money to be squandered by some young fool of a husband. I want you to marry and to marry at once my partner Pretoria Smith, as we call him. You may find him a bit rough, but he is a straight 'un. He took a lot of persuading, but because he loves his old partner he has agreed. He will be on his way when this reaches you. Cable me your decision. If you say no, Marjorie, then the large allowance I make to your mother ceases forthwith. I will wash my hands of you.

Your affectionate uncle,
SOLOMON STEDMAN

Marjorie Stedman read the letter again and the words swam before her eyes.

Those big grey eyes were set well apart in a face of delicate sweetness. Hands and feet were small but not too small for that slight figure, with its soft curves and its graceful lines.

There were few more beautiful women in the world than Marjorie Stedman, who from the crown of her golden head to the tips of her dainty shoes would have satisfied the most exigent requirements of the old Greek sculptors. The virginal purity of her flawless skin was emphasized by a pair of vivid red lips, inviting and tantalizing.

Now the ivory skin was tinted pink with shame and indignation and the lovely eyes blazed with hopeless anger.

"How dare he, how dare he!" she cried, and the rise and fall of her bosom revealed something of the emotion the letter had aroused.

She was to be married by order! She who shrank from the very idea of marriage, who at most had seen a lover as a nebulous godlike creature without substance or shape, in a golden haze of dreams, to whom marriage was an ideal rather than a possibility, was to be married by order to – Pretoria Smith!

It was only then as she repeated the name that the man came back to her mind. Pretoria Smith! For three and a half years she had by an effort of will excluded the memory of that terrible night at Tynewood Chase from her mind; though she lived within riding distance of the old family home of Tynewoods, though Alma Tynewood by the curious workings of fate was almost a daily visitor at the house, she had steadfastly kept Pretoria Smith from recollection. Was it the same man? There were many Smiths in Pretoria. He might be some wild uncouth lout whom old Solomon Stedman had picked up in the wilds of Africa. Her uncle had lived a hard life and had a reputation which her father had been loth to discuss. He had killed men and in his early days had served a sentence of penal servitude for some vague crime. She had never seen him, for the old man had lived all his life in distant lands – America, Australia, South Africa.

And yet –

When his luck had turned four years ago, his first thought had been for his dead brother's child. He had taken her from the drudgery of office work and her mother from the suburban lodgings and had bought for them their old family home where she was born. And she had been happy and had almost forgotten… The county had taken her to its heart and tomorrow was to do her honour.

Old Solomon's money had done this, she remembered, and her resentment toward him softened.

She looked at the letter again.

"He took a lot of persuading," she read, and the hot tears of humiliation filled her eyes.

41

She was to be bought and sold, bought with Solomon's money and sold to his partner – and the purchaser had to be "persuaded" to take his bargain!

She sprang to her feet, flaming with righteous anger, then a sense of sickness supervened and she sank back again on the stone seat and, covering her face with her hands, wept silently into her handkerchief.

That was the end of her rosy dream – she must go back to the grind of office work. To the crowded tubes and the packed buses, to the fogs and the drizzle, the bleak mornings and the cheerless nights, with a few hard-earnt days of holiday every year in a seaside boarding-house.

"I wonder what mother will say?" she asked herself and dried her eyes.

For a while she sat, looking across the close-mown lawn toward the dear house, all gables and angles and drooping wisteria. To the flower-beds a-riot with colour, to the pond where the ducks swam, serenely ignorant of the approaching day when the slim girl who fed them, standing on the crumbling stone edge, her figure reflected in the still water, would go away and be no more seen.

She rose with a sigh. There was no help for it. The caprice of this old man who had set them up in a fool's paradise would cast them down again. As she walked slowly across the lawn, it was of her mother she was thinking. There would be the difficult task. Her heart ached for the woman she so dearly loved, and yet whose faults and failings she saw so clearly.

And then she brightened up. For over three years they had enjoyed an income of over £4,000 a year. There would be money saved, and with that money the fall might be eased.

"Marry Pretoria Smith I will not," she said, as she opened one of the long French windows that led into the drawing-room.

She must have spoken her thought aloud, for the two women who were in the room turned before her hand closed upon the catch of the door.

It was early in the day for visitors, and when Marjorie saw who that visitor was, she would have drawn back and made her escape; but now it was too late, and she walked in with a smile which she felt was a little forced to the slim, graceful girl who rose.

"Good morning, Lady Tynewood," she said politely.

Alma Tynewood had never wholly concealed her dislike for Marjorie. But now there was a special reason for her detestation, and her lips, for the crimson of which art was to some extent responsible, curled in a malicious little smile.

Mrs Stedman, a pretty, faded woman with rather a weak face, seemed flustered by the unexpected arrival of her daughter.

"My dear, I thought you had gone riding."

"I'm riding this afternoon," said the girl.

"Lance said you had promised to go this morning."

"Mother, dear, I had so many things to do this morning," replied the girl patiently. "I am riding this afternoon; if Lance is too busy I shall go alone." And Mrs Stedman, with a discontented sigh, subsided.

"I should not have thought that you could have spared the time for riding," said Lady Tynewood with a disagreeable laugh. "My dear, aren't you spending all your days preparing the speech you are going to make tomorrow?"

"I am not making a speech," said Marjorie shortly, "and I'm sure nobody wants to hear me. I think the Committee are making a great fuss about nothing and are exaggerating the service I have rendered to the County Hospital. It is true I have collected fifty thousand pounds in the sense that I was Secretary to the Fund. But anybody could have done the same."

"Nobody is quite as fascinating as you, Miss Stedman," said Lady Tynewood unpleasantly. "If I were a man, and a beautiful girl like you came into my office and started to wheedle a subscription from me, I should immediately open my chequebook and ask you to name any sum you liked. Besides, you got a thousand pounds for a kiss, I'm told."

"That is a lie," said the girl steadily, "and nobody knows it better than you."

"Marjorie!" murmured her mother appealingly.

"My dear, it is a story that is being circulated – "

"And you circulated it," said Marjorie, "well knowing it to be a wicked invention. Lady Tynewood, I know something of you and your past, and it is probable that you moved in a circle where kisses were bought and sold, and nobody thought any worse of the buyer or the seller."

The woman's face went a dull red and her eyes flashed fire. She recovered control of her voice, however.

"The circle in which I moved," she sneered, "is one which would certainly be foreign to you, though I admit it is not as exalted as the circle in which you will move tomorrow night."

The girl bit her lip and said nothing, pretending to busy herself with some papers on the table, whilst Mrs Stedman looked hopelessly on.

"Was it your idea that the County Hospital dinner should be served tomorrow night at separate tables?" asked Lady Tynewood, scarcely disguising her rising wrath. "And that I should be excluded from the table where His Royal Highness will sit – with you on his right, I suppose?" she sneered.

It's very possible," said the girl coolly, "but at any rate I can give you some comfort by telling you that it was not my idea but Lord Wadham's. I had nothing to do with the placing of the guests, and the fact that you are excluded from the prince's table is no affair or action of mine."

"So you say," said the woman pointedly.

"I can't expect to convince you," said Marjorie, "but I don't remember having told a lie in my life. I told you, Lady Tynewood, that you were refused a seat at that table by someone who has greater authority than I."

"Where am I to sit?" asked the woman wrathfully. "Amongst the country bumpkins, the doctors and little squires of Billingham?"

The girl shrugged her shoulders.

"My dear, don't you think," asked her mother timidly "that you could induce the Committee to let Lady Tynewood sit at the Duke's table? After all, she is one of the County, and the Tynewoods are the greatest of the great families in Droitshire."

Marjorie made no reply.

"Well," asked Alma Tynewood sharply, "you heard your mother speak to you?"

"I shall answer my mother in private," said the girl, "and give her very excellent reasons for your sitting amongst country bumpkins."

The woman's lips took a straight line.

Oh, I see," she said. "It is a plot, eh?"

"Not a plot of which I have any knowledge," replied Marjorie, her face flushed and her eyes dangerously bright. "But I tell you this, Lady Tynewood – that, had they put you at my table, I should not have sat with you."

The woman drew a long breath, and with a nod to the distressed Mrs Stedman walked to the door.

"One day, my girl, I'll make you sorry for that," she said between her teeth, and with this parting shot she opened the door and slammed it behind her.

MRS STEDMAN'S TROUBLE

Mrs Stedman looked at her daughter irritably.

"My dear, you've made an enemy of Lady Tynewood," she said a little petulantly. She had also the temper of a weak woman. Mrs Stedman was not designed to be a mother or to accept responsibility. There are many mothers in the world who are as utterly unfit, and unsuited to control, to understand or to sympathize with the finer minds of their children.

"It doesn't really matter," said Marjorie hopelessly. "The enmity of Lady Tynewood is the least of my troubles."

"She has been a good friend of ours," insisted Mrs Stedman. "I'm sure your dear uncle would not like to know that you had offended a lady of title."

"Oh, mother," said the girl near to tears, "what is 'a lady of title' but a woman who has married a man who has inherited the reward of somebody else's genius? The only titles that are worth while are the titles that are earned by those who hold them."

"My dear, that sounds like high treason to me," said her mother severely. "I do wish you wouldn't get these socialistic ideas in your head."

Despite her unhappiness, the girl laughed.

"Don't let us talk of titles, mother," she said. "I have so much that is more important to discuss." She hardly knew how to begin. "Mother," she said after a pause, "you love the Priory, don't you?"

"Yes, my dear," said her mother, thinking she was trying to change the subject for her own purpose. "But I tell you that Lady Tynewood – "

"Let's leave Lady Tynewood alone for a moment," said Marjorie good-humouredly. "But, mother, there are things you like more than the Priory and this life and the comfort we enjoy?"

"I suppose so," said Mrs Stedman vaguely. "Of course, when one's thoughts are fixed on heaven – "

"I'm not even thinking about heaven, I'm thinking about the tangible things of life, the things that count," said the girl. "The honour and happiness of your daughter, for example."

Mrs Stedman looked up sharply and her underlip drooped pathetically.

"The honour of my child?" she repeated. "Oh, Marjorie, you haven't been using any of the money which you collected for the hospital, have you?"

The girl rose with a despairing gesture.

"I don't know whether to laugh or cry," she said, and walked to the window.

"Well, for goodness' sake, laugh," said Mrs Stedman, adjusting her glasses and picking up a current magazine, "for I am in very low spirits."

"Mother, suppose we had to leave here?" said Marjorie turning, "and go back to the old life?"

"Don't suggest anything so horrible," begged Mrs Stedman with a shiver. "I should not survive a week of it. Thanks to the generosity and kindness of your dear Uncle Solomon, we need never fear want or hardship again, my love."

"But suppose we had to," said the girl desperately.

"I won't suppose anything so awful," snapped Mrs Stedman. "Now, Marjorie, you're being very trying, and my heart is not all it should be. Do you want to make me ill? I did hope to find you in a sympathetic mood today," she wailed. "I've got something I want to tell you."

"To tell me?" said the girl slowly with a sense of apprehension. "But perhaps I'd better tell you first," she went on. "Mother, how much money have we saved in the past four years?"

"Saved!" almost screamed the woman. "Saved, Marjorie? Are you mad?"

The girl looked at her aghast.

"Do you mean to say we haven't saved anything?" she demanded. "Out of four thousand a year – sixteen thousand pounds? We've had no rent to pay, no garden produce to buy, nothing but the servants' wages and the meat and coal. Haven't you saved any money?" she asked, with an awful quaking of heart.

Mrs Stedman shook her head and two tears rolled down her cheeks.

"No, my dear," she gulped. "I haven't saved any money. I am five hundred pounds overdrawn at the bank, and – and – and – " and she began to sob.

"And?" said the girl relentlessly. "Tell me the worst, mother, please."

Her face was white as death, and the hand she brought to smooth back her hair shook as with an ague.

"I owe thousands of pounds," blurted Mrs Stedman hysterically.

Marjorie dropped into the nearest chair.

"Don't look at me like that," her mother went on. "Oh dear, I wish I'd never had children sometimes! You've never been a comfort to me, Marjorie, when I need comforting most."

At last the girl found her voice, and a shaky voice it was.

"Mother, dear," she asked, "to whom do you owe thousands of pounds?"

"To Lady Tynewood," sniffed Mrs Stedman, "and I don't see why you should ask me questions, Marjorie. I'm your own mother, and it's disrespectful of you. It's against all the teachings of the Book to cross-examine your own mother about her money!"

The girl looked out of the window. So that was what it meant! Those long afternoon visits which Mrs Stedman paid to Monk House, Alma Tynewood's little estate. No wonder Lady Tynewood had sent her car for this much flattered lady!

"I suppose you have played bridge with Lady Tynewood?" said Marjorie quietly. "And Mr Javot. Who was the fourth?"

"We didn't have a fourth," whimpered Mrs Stedman. "We played double-dummy. And, Marjorie, I had such luck at first; I won nearly a thousand pounds. And then the luck steadily began to go against me and I lost and lost. But dear Alma was most kind, Marjorie. You must never misjudge her; she has been a very good friend of mine. Never once has she asked me for repayment, although I know her own income isn't a very great one."

Marjorie rose and came across to her mother and patted her gently on the shoulder.

"Mother, you mustn't play again," she said, "because we can't afford it."

"I shall win it all back one of these days," said Mrs Stedman eagerly. "You've no idea what atrocious cards I've been holding – "

"I have some idea," said the girl with a hard smile, "if Alma Tynewood was playing against you."

Should she tell her mother about the letter that had come? What use would it be? What help or comfort could she get from this woman who absorbed help and comfort as sand absorbs water, and gave nothing back? Thousands of pounds! And her income would stop next week! It would kill her mother, she knew that. Kill her as assuredly as if she took that Oriental knife from the wall and plunged it into her heart. She licked her dry lips and stood looking down at the shaking figure, huddled up in the big armchair.

"Never mind, mother dear," she said gently. "After all, I dare say we can manage somehow. The house is worth quite a big sum."

"The house? What utter rubbish you talk!" said Mrs Stedman, forgetting in her indignation her pose of woe. "You don't imagine we should sell the house or mortgage it? Anyway, I've already mortgaged it," she said defiantly.

The girl, who thought she was impervious to shock, nearly collapsed.

"You've mortgaged it!" she said faintly. "But, dear, it's not yours to mortgage. It belongs to uncle."

"He gave it to us," snorted Mrs Stedman. "He gave it to me! I've a right to do what I like with it. You are very, very trying, Marjorie, and just when I wanted you to write to your dear uncle, who is so fond of you, and ask him if he could lend us a little. You could easily tell him that you were going to be married, or something."

"Going to be married!" repeated the girl, laughing hysterically.

Then, to Mrs Stedman's amazement, she ran from the room and the mother heard her feet upon the stairs and the slam of her bedroom door and the snap of the lock as she turned the key.

MARJORIE SENDS HER WIRE

The young man waiting at the entrance of the drive in smart riding-kit was good-looking in an effeminate way. His fair hair was brushed neatly back over the top of his head, and was brightly brilliantined; his nails were daintily manicured; and his hands, of which he was inordinately proud, were white and graceful. One of these rose to lift his hat in a sweeping salute as Marjorie, dressed for walking, came through the gate.

"Hullo, Marjorie," he said, "I thought you were riding this morning?"

Lance Kelman was her cousin, the son of her mother's brother. He was a young man who possessed unbounded confidence in himself, a confidence which he had hoped to impose upon Solomon Stedman – for Lance had taken his adventurous trip to South Africa hoping for a nice, fat job where the work was done by somebody else, or preferably a handsome settlement upon himself by virtue of his distant relationship.

In all his expectations he had been disappointed. His views upon Solomon Stedman, as Marjorie knew, were neither flattering nor charitable. Marjorie had not intended discussing the matter with her cousin, but she felt now that she must talk it over with somebody or she would go mad.

She wanted strength, just a little additional strength, to meet this supreme crisis in her young life.

"Yes, yes," she said hastily, "I am riding this afternoon."

"I thought of taking you over to Tynewood Chase," he said.

He had a way of talking as though he owned the country and was its principal showman; but today his little conceit did not amuse her, and she made a wry face.

"I don't know that I want to see anything associated with the Tynewoods today," she said. "You're coming to the dinner tomorrow, Lance?"

He nodded, but with a little frown.

"I wonder you didn't manage to get me at the table with you, Marjorie," he said complainingly. "I don't want to hobnob with royalty, but I should rather like to have been near you. And what's the matter with Lady Tynewood?" he asked quickly. "You haven't been quarrelling again?"

"I haven't been quarrelling; she did all that," said Marjorie, "and it was on the same subject – a place at the high table at tomorrow's dinner. I wish I wasn't going to the dinner."

"Isn't she there either?" asked Lance.

"No, she's not," snapped the girl, whose nerves were on edge, "and I am very glad. I have nothing to do with the placing of people at the tables, high or low."

He was ruffled for the same reason as Lady Tynewood, and made her case his own.

She isn't a bad sort, believe me," he said. "She's a pretty knowledgeable woman of the world, and I've a great respect for her. It's nothing like the feeling I've got for you, mark you, dear," he added.

"I am going to the village now, Lance," she said, impatient to be gone. "Will you be ready at two o'clock? You look so nice in your riding-suit," she smiled, "that I don't think I should change."

He smiled a little complacently.

"All right, two o'clock. But can't I go with you into the village?"

She shook her head.

"No, I'm going to the post office to do some business," she said, "and I'd rather go alone."

She did not wait for him to urge his attendance upon her, but turned with a nod and walked quickly down the hill to the straggling village of Tynewood.

Tynewood, Tynewood! How she detested the name! Though she had had little but happiness in this neighbourhood since she had come. But somehow Alma Tynewood's presence poisoned the sweetness of life; and now the woman had her mother in her clutches, and had forced her to a course against which her soul and her conscience revolted. At that moment she hated Lady Tynewood most heartily.

Everything conspired against her that morning. The post office lay at the farther end of the one street, through which she very seldom passed, for the railway station was two miles away in the direction from whence she had come. As she hurried through, Perkins, the butcher, slipped out of his shop and came up to her apologetically touching his cap.

"I'm sorry to bother you, Miss Stedman," he said, "and I have been trying to see you for a fortnight past."

"Trying to see me?" said Marjorie in surprise. "What do you want to see me about?"

"Well, miss," said the man uncomfortably, "I never like dunning a customer like you, especially when you're so highly respected in the County, but I do wish your lady mother would settle that little account of mine."

Marjorie's heart sank.

"Does she owe you much?" she asked.

"A hundred and twenty pounds, miss," said the butcher. "It may not be much to her, but it's quite a lot to a man like me, and with the bills falling due, I'm rather hard put to it to find ready money just now."

Marjorie bit her lip.

"All right, Mr Perkins," she said, "I will see that your bill is settled."

She had hardly gone a dozen paces before she found little Mr Grain waiting for her. Mr Grain was the local builder.

"Miss Stedman," he said as awkwardly as the butcher, "would it be asking you too much to remind your mother that my bill hasn't been settled? It is nearly twelve months old. You remember I did a lot of repairs to your house and painted the place inside and out last spring."

"Is it much?" she asked unsteadily.

"About a hundred and eighty pounds, miss. I've written to your mother, but she has never replied."

"I'll see to it, Mr Grain," said the girl. "Mother has been very busy of late, and it must have escaped her memory."

She felt sick at the thought that almost every one of these poor little tradesmen, who had as much as they could do to make both ends meet, were creditors of her mother. If she needed any stiffening in her purpose, it was supplied in these sordid details.

She walked into the post office with her head held high and took a yellow telegraph form from a heap on the counter.

"That's a foreign form, miss," said the postmistress.

"I know," replied Marjorie.

Somehow she could not bring herself to write, but presently, with an effort, she dipped the nib in the ink and wrote, addressing the telegram to "Solomon Stedman, Stedman's Mine, Vrykloof, South Africa." Again she stopped, incapable of proceeding, and then, with a sudden resolution, she wrote:

"I accept Pretoria Smith," and signed in a bold hand: "Marjorie Stedman."

MARJORIE TELLS THE NEWS

"What is the matter with Marjorie?" asked Lance Kelman lazily, as he struck a match to light his cigarette.

Mrs Stedman held out her thin hands in a gesture which was intended to signify her complete ignorance.

"I never can understand Marjorie, and the older she gets the farther she seems to draw away from me," she complained. "She hasn't sympathy with me, Lance. She doesn't understand the requirements of my temperament."

"She's very young," said Lance condescendingly; "perhaps if she travelled a little more, her mind would broaden and she'd understand things better."

Mrs Stedman never lacked understanding from her nephew, and she looked admiringly at his trim figure.

"I wish Marjorie would settle down, Lance," she said. "I sometimes wish she would marry. Do you know what I was hoping when you went out to South Africa to see dear Solomon – it was very brave of you to take that terrible journey? I was wishing that Solomon would make your fortune and that you would come back in a position to marry."

"To marry Marjorie, you mean?" said Lance, by no means overwhelmed at the prospect. "Yes, I had some idea of that myself. She's a dear girl," he added, "though somewhat narrow in view, auntie."

"Exactly my idea," said Mrs Stedman, glancing nervously at the clock. "How long will Marjorie be, I wonder?"

"Are you going out this afternoon, auntie?" asked Lance.

"I did think of going," said Mrs Stedman, lowering her voice, "but I beg of you not to mention the fact to Marjorie. She has an unreasonable prejudice against Lady Tynewood."

"You're going to the Tynewoods', eh?" said her nephew. "Well, I agree with you. Lady Tynewood is a real good sort. I was telling her about my troubles the other day, and she asked me if I'd ever met her husband – Sir James Tynewood, you know. He ran away from her, I believe, though I've never got the story right."

"There is a lot of gossip," began Mrs Stedman, when her discourse was interrupted by the arrival of Marjorie. The girl looked exquisite in her riding-suit. A perfectly fitting long grey coat hung to where the tall polished riding-boots met the knee of the wellcut breeches, and Lance looked at her admiringly.

"For a prude, Marje, you sometimes dress very daringly."

"I am not a prude, and please don't call me Marje," said Marjorie. "It sounds like the stuff we used to spread on our bread in Brixton."

"My dear," reproved Mrs Stedman with a shiver, "don't let us refer to those horrible times."

The girl sighed.

"Are you ready?" she asked, and without waiting for a reply walked out to where the horses were waiting. He hurried to her assistance, but she had put her foot in the stirrup and had swung herself to the saddle before he could touch her.

"You're mighty independent," he grumbled, and was considerably annoyed because he rather prided himself on the manner in which he could handle a lady in those circumstances.

They passed through a long, narrow lane with high hedgerows, and Marjorie did not speak for some time. She intended telling Lance just what she had done, and she did not doubt what his opinion would be.

"Your mother was talking about Tynewood," and the girl groaned inwardly.

"I hope she's not going to the Tynewoods' this afternoon," she said suddenly, but Lance did not enlighten her.

"You have never seen the Chase, have you?"

She had been to Tynewood Chase. She recalled the circumstances with a shiver.

"I have never seen the place," she answered truthfully.

"It's a beautiful old Tudor building with a magnificent park. How a man can be content to leave a lovely wife and an estate of this kind and wander in the wilderness, heaven only knows!"

"You are speaking of Sir James Tynewood?" she asked slowly, and he nodded.

"Yes. He left his wife, you know, a few days after they were married. The real story is not known locally. Sir James has two estates, and he spent most of his time on the other. Indeed, there's nobody attached to the Chase, except the old gatekeeper, who knows him. He married about four years ago, quite unexpectedly. Lady Tynewood had been on the stage, you know."

"I heard something of that," she said quietly.

"I think he must have been mad," said Lance. "Left her, my dear, without a minute's warning. He married in London – "

"Who told you all this?" asked the girl.

"Well, to be perfectly candid, Lady Tynewood told me the very sad story of her life, or a portion of it, when I was taking tea there the other day," said Lance with a show of indifference.

"I see," said the girl with an inward smile. "Go on, please. I am very much interested in Sir James Tynewood. In fact, it's the only Tynewood thing that does interest me."

"He went away," continued Lance, a little proud to know the story at first hand. "They married suddenly in London, and he was rather a wild sort of fellow, as far as I can judge, and got into several scrapes before he met Alma – I mean Lady Tynewood. I remember – I was at Winchester at the time – the papers were full of it, and one of them happened to mention the fact that Lady Tynewood would now be the proud wearer of the famous Tynewood collar – that's a collar of diamonds, you know."

".I didn't think it was a dog's collar," she said without a smile, and he looked at her suspiciously.

"Well, she insisted on James getting this for her, and he came down here to Tynewood Chase, and from that moment" – he paused dramatically – "he was never seen again. The next morning Lady Tynewood received a letter from his lawyer, saying that, although James was married to her, she must not under any circumstances enter the doors of the Chase. A sum of money was settled on her – quite inadequate, my dear, for a woman of her position – and the next thing she knew was to read an announcement that James Tynewood had left for South Africa."

"South Africa?" said the girl quickly. "Oh, of course, the *Carisbroohe Castle* goes to South Africa, doesn't it?"

"I didn't say anything about the ship," said Lance, satisfied that he had created a sensation and not troubling to ask (this to the girl's relief) how she associated the mail boat with the lost Sir James. "But why did you say 'South Africa' in that curious tone?"

"Because I am interested in South Africa," she said, and her voice was hard, so hard that he turned and looked at her in surprise. "I am going to marry Pretoria Smith!"

"Pretoria Smith!" he gasped. "What do you mean?"

"Read this."

She took the letter from her pocket and handed it to him, and he reined in his horse and read the letter through.

"But you're not going to do a thing like this?" he said. "Pretoria Smith – I know the brute! A bullying, nigger-whacking ruffian. Why, I saw him flog an unfortunate native till I had to interfere. He was in the courts once for shooting a bushman named – anyway, I forget his name, but he was in the courts. And he drinks! I've seen him reeling about the town. They say – "

"Oh don't, don't!" she said with a shudder, and covered her eyes with her hands.

"It's not true, Marjorie. You're not going to do it. My dear, I was hoping and praying for the day when I could ask you myself to be my wife."

She stopped him with a gesture.

"I could never be your wife," she said quietly. "Don't let that complication enter into a business which is already horribly tangled."

"But it's impossible!" he cried. "It's madness. I will not allow it."

She smiled bitterly.

"Unfortunately you cannot prevent it," she said. "I have to do it."

She did not tell him the story of her mother's folly, of her own tragic misery, and they rode on, he smouldering with rage and feeling a personal grievance, she with a feeling of helplessness in face of the inevitable. And so they came to the gates of the Chase and reined in.

"I don't feel like looking over the place today," said the girl wearily.

She could see from where she sat the natural beauty of the park, the tall, spreading trees, the grey, aged building standing in dignity with its mullioned windows gleaming in the light of the afternoon sun.

"Let us stay here. I want to retain this picture. It is very beautiful," she said softly.

And for a while the loveliness of the scene put her own trouble out of her mind. Whilst they sat they heard the whirr of a motor car, and a long-bonneted limousine came into view, and stopped opposite the gates, and a lady got out.

"Lady Tynewood," whispered Lance, and the girl was going to turn her horse, but feminine curiosity got the better of her.

Lady Tynewood walked up to the gates and the liveried porter opened them and stood in the opening.

"Is there anything I can do for your ladyship?" he asked, touching his hat.

"I want to see over the grounds," said Lady Tynewood, but the man did not move.

"I'm very sorry, my lady, but I have orders that you are not under any circumstances to be admitted."

"And you have orders from me to stand on one side," she cried in a fury. "I have been too long obedient to the wishes of your employer. I insist upon my right to enter the grounds as and when I wish."

For answer he stepped back and gently closed the gates in her face.

"I'm very sorry, my lady," he said between the bars. "My orders are strict. I cannot allow you to enter."

The woman turned away in a towering rage and came face to face with Marjorie.

"You!" she said, and her voice was hoarse. She put her hand to her throat as though she had some difficulty in breathing, and then: "This is another humiliation you have witnessed, Marjorie Stedman," she said, breathing heavily. "I have two scores to wipe out with you."

Marjorie said nothing for a moment, then: "You may wipe out any scores you have, Lady Tynewood," she said softly, "but they will never be bridge scores!"

And she turned her horse's head and rode away.

THE MAN WHO WAS NOBODY

Mr Vance, of that eminent firm of solicitors, Vance & Vance, was in the midst of a busy day's work when a visitor was announced, and as he read the card his eyebrows rose.

"Show Miss Stedman in, please."

He got up and came halfway across the room to meet her.

"Why, this is a most unexpected pleasure, Miss Stedman," he said, closing the door after her. "You haven't come for legal advice, I hope?"

"No, not exactly that," she replied with a little smile.

"I have heard great stories of your progress in the county," said Mr Vance. "Sit down there, my dear. Why, it's good to see you again. I shall never have another secretary like you. Yes, I hear great things about you; you raised a lot of money for the County Hospital, I'm told. And isn't there a complimentary dinner to you soon, or has it gone past?"

"It is not exactly a complimentary dinner to me," she smiled. "I think it is to be a function where everybody congratulates themselves, and I am to be one of the complacent many.

"Mr Vance," she said, her voice striking a more serious note. "did you ever know Uncle Solomon?"

"I think I told you I'd met him," replied Vance, nodding. "I have only the dimmest recollection of Mr Stedman."

"You know he has made a very large fortune?"

He nodded again.

"You told me that in your letter and I congratulate you all. What is the matter?" he asked quickly. "Has he lost his money?"

She shook her head.

61

"Sometimes I almost wish he had," she said ruefully. "No, he has done no more than" – she hesitated – "attempt to shape my life."

He looked a little puzzled, then a light dawned upon him.

"Has he chosen a husband for you?" he asked with a twinkle in his eyes.

"You have guessed rightly," she said quietly.

"And who's the lucky man?"

"Somebody you know very well," she answered.

The half smile vanished from the lawyer's face.

"Somebody I know? You're quite mysterious, Miss Stedman. Is it a friend of mine?"

"I don't know whether he's a friend of yours, but he's somebody I have met in this office – Mr Smith from Pretoria."

He half rose from his seat, a look of incredulity on his face.

"Mr Smith of Pretoria? Impossible!" he replied.

"I wish it were," she said, amused in spite of herself at his evident perturbation, and a little troubled too.

Briefly she related all the circumstances. The arrival of her uncle's letter, and her conversation with her mother. It was not a time when she could afford to respect the confidences of the older woman, and she spoke frankly of Mrs Stedman's weakness.

"You leave me breathless," said the lawyer when she had finished. "I had no idea that Mr Smith was in England."

He pondered a moment, and the girl watched his face, noting the evident emotion which her announcement had caused.

"There is one question I want to ask you, Mr Vance, and I beg of you to answer me truthfully – that sounds very rude, but such great issues are at stake for me that I must have the truth."

"What is the question you wish to ask?" he demanded quietly.

"I want to know this," she said, speaking with deliberation. "What was the meaning of that scene I witnessed at Tynewood Chase four years ago?"

He was silent.

"I cannot answer that question, Miss Stedman," he said at last. "I am sorry, but to answer that would be to betray the confidence of a friend. It would mean, too, the disgracing of a very old name."

"The name of Tynewood?" she said quickly, and he nodded.

"Then perhaps you will answer another question," said the girl. "If I marry Pretoria Smith, am I marrying the man who has caused Sir James Tynewood to disappear from England – I do not say murdered him," she added quickly, "that is too dreadful a possibility. Though I know Sir James Tynewood is dead, yet I have been faithful to my promise to you that I would never speak of the events I saw at Tynewood Chase."

He nodded. There was a look of quiet respect in his eyes.

"I am indeed grateful to you, Miss Stedman," he said, "and when Sir James returns from his retirement he also will be grateful."

She looked at him steadily.

"Sir James Tynewood is dead," she said, and his eyes narrowed.

"I repeat," he answered evenly, "that when Sir James Tynewood comes back from his retirement, he will be grateful to you."

The girl came a little nearer to the table and dropped her clasped hands on the desk.

"I'm going to be open and honest with you, Mr Vance," she said. "I know Sir James Tynewood is dead. By accident I came into your room when you were discussing his death with Dr Fordham."

The old lawyer rose from his chair and paced the room slowly, his chin upon his breast, his hands clasped behind him. Suddenly he stopped opposite to her.

"Are you going to marry Pretoria Smith?" he asked.

She shrugged her shoulders.

"What else am I to do?"

He rubbed his chin thoughtfully.

"You might do worse, much worse," he said with emphasis. "Pretoria Smith is a very decent man and comes of a good family."

"Is his name Smith?" she asked.

"Is anybody's name Smith?" he answered good-humouredly. "Now, now, Miss Stedman" – he dropped his hand on her shoulder – "won't you take the advice of an old friend?"

"What is your advice?"

"Marry Pretoria Smith!" was the astonishing answer.

"Marry a drunkard!" she said scornfully.

"A drunkard!" he gaped at her in amazement. "Pretoria Smith a drunkard?" he said incredulously. "Why, Miss Stedman, what do you mean?"

"My cousin, Lance Kelman, was in South Africa, and knows the man perhaps better than you do," she said. "He told me he had often seen Pretoria Smith staggering about the town the worse for drink."

She was annoyed with her old employer and irritated and shocked at the suggestion that she should marry Pretoria Smith, and she was dismally triumphant at the look of blank consternation on the lawyer's face.

"Will you tell me, Mr Vance," she went on, "what is his name? Obviously I cannot marry a man whose name I do not know."

He hesitated and scratched his chin irresolutely and was obviously embarrassed.

"If I tell you," he said, speaking slowly, "I shall extract from you a promise that you will not tell either Pretoria Smith or any other person that I have given you this information."

"I can promise that," she said at once.

"His name," he said slowly, "is Norman Garrick."

"Norman Garrick," she repeated; then, as a sudden inspiration came to her, "Was he any relation of – of the young man who is dead?"

She felt the name of "Tynewood" would choke her at that moment. Again the lawyer paused.

"He is his half brother," he said in a low voice, "and that is all I can tell you."

Mr Vance spoke of her life in the country and the forthcoming dinner, and then she took her leave of the lawyer. In the outer office she stopped to speak to the managing clerk, an old friend of hers, and went into his room.

"Quite like old times seeing you again, Miss Stedman," he chuckled. "We haven't had anybody at the office quite as pleasant to work with as yourself."

"If you're busy," she laughed, "I'll come along and help you."

"I wish to goodness you would," he grumbled. "I have got heaps and heaps of estate matters to file."

In truth his desk was choked with an accumulation of papers and bundles of papers.

"You always were untidy, Mr Herman," she said, and mechanically began to set them in order as she had done so often.

As she stacked the folded documents on one side of the table her eyes fell upon a little bundle tied with red tape and this she took up to place it with the others she was piling. Mechanically she read:

"In the matter of Norman Garrick."

She dropped the bundle with a little cry and stared at the managing clerk.

"Who is Norman Garrick?" she asked desperately.

The managing clerk looked at her with an odd expression and reaching out took the bundle from the heap and dropped it into a drawer.

"One of our clients," he said indifferently, "or at least he was. He's been dead some time now."

Two minutes later she was walking down the stairs of the office, her brain in a whirl.

Pretoria Smith was Norman Garrick – and Norman Garrick was dead! Who then was Pretoria Smith? He was a man who was – nobody!

HIS ROYAL HIGHNESS

It was the night of the great dinner which the Board of Management of the Droitshire County Hospital were giving to celebrate the raising of the funds which had been necessary for the continuance of the hospital's work. In reality it was a dinner in honour of the energetic secretary of the fund, the girl who had worked with unremitting energy to make the fund a success.

Marjorie Stedman had utilized the knowledge she had gained in a London office, and had engrafted to that a natural sweetness of appeal and a natural genius for organization which had done so much to produce the required sum.

His Royal Highness the Duke of Wight, who was President of the hospital, had come down from London to preside, and was the guest of the Earl of Wadham, who had his seat in the neighbourhood. In the excitement and thrill of the brilliant gathering, at which every county family was represented, Marjorie, looking exquisite in a gown of silver and white, managed to forget the disturbing events of the previous day and stood the smiling recipient of congratulations from the guests which crowded the County Hall.

Lord Wadham, white-haired and red-faced, with a ready smile and a monocle, pushed his way through the throng to Marjorie's side.

"Oh, here you are," he said loudly. He had a voice like a foghorn and his whispers were audible on the other side of the street. "Come along, Miss Stedman. I want to present you to His Royal Highness."

He made his way through the press of people to the farther end of the reception room, where, standing aloof with two or three gentlemen about him, was the slight, boyish figure of the Duke of Wight, the blue band of the Garter over his snowy shirt-front.

"Your Royal Highness, may I present Miss Marjorie Stedman, who has done so much for the Droitshire Hospital?"

The Duke smiled and held out his hand.

"I have heard of you, Miss Stedman," he said, "and I want to thank you personally. I have a great interest in this hospital and in its prosperity, and I feel that, but for your energy and your tireless work, our appeal might have failed."

She curtsied and smiled as she took his hand.

"Your Royal Highness doesn't realize what a pleasure it was to work for the hospital," she said.

"My Royal Highness recognizes what a pleasure it must be to work with you, who are working for the hospital," said the Prince good-naturedly, and looked at Lord Wadham and then at his watch. At that moment a footman announced that dinner was served, and they moved to the big inner room.

Dinner was to be served at separate tables. There were fifty small tables that covered the whole of the floor space, and at the farther end a larger table, decorated with greenery and glittering with silver; and it was to this that Marjorie was led on the royal arm.

"You're on my right," he said, and she sat down, conscious of the envious and the amused eyes which were cast in her direction.

For the old gentry, which had made the county what it was, her elevation to honour was only a source of gratification and pleasure; it was the little folk, the successful profiteers, who hated her, and to these might be added Lady Tynewood, who saw the girl's triumph from a table halfway down the room and loathed her. She turned to her companion.

"Well, Mr Lance Kelman, what do you think of your cousin?"

"Oh, she's all right," said Lance Kelman, who had learnt that it was impolitic to speak well of Marjorie before this overawing lady and in consequence did not consider it disloyal to disparage her. "She's bound to get a little swollen-headed," he added tolerantly. "Young people always do."

She looked at him with amusement.

"I don't think you're so very old, are you?" she said sarcastically. "So she's going to marry a miner in South Africa, eh? Pretoria Smith."

"A perfect brute," said Lance violently. "By Jove, if she could only see him as I saw him, she'd chuck him up at once! She's a weak fool anyway, and I'd give anything to teach her a lesson."

The girl was not thinking of Pretoria Smith or of anybody. The Prince was talking to her about the hospital, when suddenly his eyes lighted on Alma.

"Isn't that Lady Tynewood?" he asked.

"Yes, sir," said the girl. "Do you know her?"

"I knew her husband," said the Prince thoughtfully. "He and I were at Eton together and we were on a couple of shooting expeditions. A real good fellow." He shook his head. "I could never understand that extraordinary marriage." And then, remembering that scandal and gossip are forbidden to members of his family, he changed the subject.

Lady Tynewood had seen the Prince's eye fall on her, and guessed, with a woman's quiet instinct, that it was not a friendly gaze.

"Lance," she said familiarly, "will you go out into the vestibule? I left my bag there and I brought a small pair of opera glasses. As I paid for the dinner, I might as well have a good look at His Royal Nibs."

Lance was only amused at the vulgarity and he obeyed. The hall was deserted, and the woman in charge of the ladies' cloaks easily found the bag and handed it to him.

He was returning to the room when his attention was attracted by the sight of a man who stood unsteadily in the middle of the vestibule. He looked again and his heart stood still for a moment, and then a great scheme was born to his mind. A malicious scheme, the consequence of which he could not foresee. The man in the hall was tall and broad-shouldered; his face, clean-shaven, was strong and almost expressionless, as though he wore a mask to hide his inmost feelings. He was dressed in a shabby reach-me-down suit such as a veld store might produce at a minute's notice and he wore a shirt with a soft collar which was open at the throat.

Lance crammed Lady Tynewood's bag in his pocket and stepped up to the man.

"Hullo!" he said, and the stranger turned slowly to meet his eyes.

"Hullo!" he replied, and his voice was a little husky.

"You're Pretoria Smith, aren't you?"

The man swayed to and fro and when he spoke it was in a lazy drawl.

"That's my name," was the reply. "Who the devil are you?"

"Don't you remember? I'm Mr Solomon Stedman's nephew."

"Oh yes, I remember," said the other, nodding. "Then perhaps you'll tell me where is the hotel. I've strayed in here, thinking this was it, but there seems to be some sort of function on."

And then the idea took shape and Lance Kelman forgot discretion, forgot what would be the consequence of his impertinence, and gripped Pretoria Smith by the arm.

"Come on," he said eagerly. "I know a side way which will bring you quite close to the person you are seeking."

"Wait a minute," said Pretoria Smith. "What is the game?"

"You're hungry, aren't you?"

"I am," said Pretoria Smith thickly after a little pause, "and I'm not. I'm more thirsty."

He swayed on his feet as he stood.

"Drunk," thought Kelman exultantly. "Now, Marjorie, I will show you the kind of man you're going to marry."

"I'll take you where you can get a drink – anything you want," he said, and took him along the side passage which ran parallel with the dining-hall.

There were several doors used for exits when entertainments were given and at the last of these he stopped. He guessed it would be opposite the high table, and would produce the greatest sensation. He had some difficulty in unlocking the door, but presently he succeeded; and led the man in, in full view of every person in the hall.

The Prince looked round with a frown and a little start. Marjorie gazed with amazement on the man she had not seen for four years and instinct warned her that he was drunk and she went pale. A momentary silence had fallen on the hall at the sight of this extraordinary intruder, and it was Lance Kelman who broke the spell.

"Your Royal Highness, Ladies and Gentlemen," he cried, "permit me to introduce you to the fiancé of Marjorie Stedman – Pretoria Smith!"

The man at his side looked round with half-closed eyes as though he were dazed, then stumbled and lurched forward toward where the Prince was standing, and the frightened girl, half-fainting, shrank back in her chair.

"Drunk, by God! "said Lord Wadham, as Pretoria Smith fell with a crash against the table, face to face with His Royal Highness.

THE INTRUDER

All her life Marjorie Stedman would retain in her mind that picture of horror and humiliation. The great room, lit by hundreds of lights, the wails draped with flags, the white tables flashing back the rays of the lamps, the pink faces turned to hers – and there, near at hand – and she shivered in a panic of fear – the sprawling figure of Pretoria Smith.

He was talking some weird, outlandish gibberish, talking fiercely as a drunken man will talk who is half conscious and half bemused; and above all, the serene figure of the Prince, standing with both his hands on the table, his head slightly bent, his unwavering eyes fixed upon the wreck before him.

It was the Prince who made the first move. Slipping round the table before the attendants could reach him, he had lifted Pretoria Smith to his feet, and, waving aside the attendants, it was be who half led, half supported the man into the hall.

And then the babble of talk began, and every face and eye was fixed on the shrinking girl, who sat frozen, tortured, humiliated to the last degree, not daring to meet any of the eyes that were turned in her direction. Presently the Prince came back, calmly, leisurely, and sat down by the girl's side. He bent over to her and patted her hand.

"My dear girl," he said in a low voice, "I am awfully sorry – who was the man who brought him in?"

He looked round and his keen eyes sought out the scared face of Lance Kelman, and he beckoned him forward. The moment Lance Kelman had accomplished his dramatic introduction, he had fallen into a blue funk; and as the Prince's finger crooked, he came forward with wobbling knees, and stood in the place where Pretoria Smith had stood.

"I don't know your name, sir," said the Duke of Wight, fixing his eye upon the young man," and I have not asked, for I do not want to know it. I can only tell you, sir, that your conduct has unfitted you for association with gentlemen, and I will ask you to retire."

Lance Kelman went out of the room, looking neither left nor right, boiling with rage which was half fear, and wildly apprehensive of what might follow. He, Lance Kelman, a man of considerable means, and a possible candidate for Parliament, had been publicly rebuked. He could have cried, and was near to tears of self-pity when he threw himself into his car and was whirled away to the house he had rented for the summer.

Few people had seen him go or realized why he went. Marjorie had heard the words, and in some way felt the reflected reproach of them; and the Duke must have realized this, for he turned to her with a smile.

"Now, Miss Stedman, you are eating nothing and you are drinking nothing," he said gaily, "and I must insist upon your doing both."

Her hand as she raised the wine-glass to her lips was shaking, and this he noticed.

"It was very dreadful for you, and I'm very sorry," he said. "That person I have just sent home is a most unutterable little cad, and I suppose he had some reason?"

"I can't divine it," said the girl with a shake of her head. "Lance and I are quite good friends, but he is piqued, I think, by something which happened."

Very gently and with rare tact the young Duke drew from her the whole of the story. The letter she had received that morning from her uncle, her aversion to the match and her horror of it. She did not tell him of their earlier meeting nor of her mother's indiscretions, but he guessed there was some vital reason why she should have accepted the nominee of Solomon Stedman.

"I had no idea that he was in England," she said. "My uncle's letter merely said that he was on his way. He must have come by the same boat as the letter."

The Prince nodded.

"What can I do, sir?" she asked helplessly. "My own inclination is to go away back to London and find some work. But there are – there are reasons why I cannot do this, and why I must accept" – she paused at the word – "Pretoria Smith and all that Pretoria Smith means."

The young Prince was silent. The room saw the conversation; not one move escaped the guests. Suddenly they saw the royal Duke rise, and the noise of talking ceased. Was he going to make some statement which would explain this most curious interruption to the dinner? Their doubts were soon to be set at rest.

"Gentlemen," said the Duke of Wight, "I give you the toast of the King."

So nothing was to be said, and they must draw their own conclusions and discover, as best they could, what was the meaning of the extraordinary scene.

Marjorie was not engaged to any man, so far as they knew, and certainly she was not the type of girl who would marry an ill-clad ruffian who was in the habit of making such an exhibition of himself.

There were a dozen men in the county who would have been happy to have led Marjorie to the altar. She had friends innumerable, and these were grieved and shocked. Incidentally, there were a few young men in that hall who registered a vow to seek out Mr Lance Kelman at the earliest opportunity and impress upon him the iniquity of his proceeding.

Presently the memory of the incident passed, the speeches began and Marjorie listened like a girl in a dream to the praise which was lavished upon her by the Prince. And then, in face of that great gathering, he pinned upon her breast the insignia of the Order of the Royal Red Cross. The cheers were deafening and spontaneous. Lady Tynewood did not cheer. Through her little jewelled glasses she was watching the scene at the table, and her lips curled in scorn.

"The man must be in love with her himself," she said aloud, "to countenance such a disgraceful scene."

Her neighbour, a stiff-backed squire, looked at her under his beetling brows.

"That is not a comment I like to hear, madam," he said, and moved farther away.

She took no notice of the rebuke. Her busy, scheming mind was wholly engaged on one matter – how best could she use Pretoria Smith, whose face she had seen for the first time in her life.

MRS STEDMAN HEARS THE NEWS

Lord Wadham drove Marjorie home that night. He was full of good cheer and roared his enthusiasm into her deafened ear.

"A great chap, the Prince," he shouted. "One of the right sort. When you have men like that at the head of affairs, you need not fear revolution or anarchy. You behaved splendidly, my girl, splendidly! I've never seen a lady in this land who could have kept her face as you did in such circumstances. I think you're just wonderful."

The girl smiled faintly, and her hand lightly touched the glittering ornament at her breast. To say that she had not been gratified and had not experienced a thrill when this honour was paid to her, would be to say that she was not human. Later, perhaps, in the sleepless hours of the night, she would think of Pretoria Smith and come to a full understanding of the insult that had been put upon her. For the moment she let her mind dwell upon more pleasant things.

"Kelman's a fool," boomed Lord Wadham. "I'm perfectly sure that he couldn't have done that by himself. That infernal Tynewood woman must have put him up to it. A bad egg, that, my dear, a damned bad egg!"

There were times when Lord Wadham's language was violent and strong. But the girl did not resent such expressions at this moment. Rather she was prepared to endorse them and be thankful to Lord Wadham for expressing her own inmost thoughts.

The car stopped at the drive and he saw her up to the door and left her. Until she got into the drawing-room she carried herself bravely; but once out of the sight of Wadham, the utter misery of her position brought a little collapse. She sat down on a settee, weary and hurt and utterly sick of everything. Mrs Stedman bustled in at the wrong moment, and was in a chirpy, cheerful mood.

"Well, my dear, how did everything go off?" she babbled. "I'm sure you were a great success in that gown. I wish your poor, dear father could have seen you. I don't like silver on white; it is a little too theatrical to please me, but girls have changed extraordinarily since I was young. And was the Prince nice to you?"

Marjorie roused herself with an effort.

"He gave me this," she said, and indicated the decoration on her bodice.

Mrs Stedman was properly impressed. "Did he really, my dear? How very nice of him!" she said. "Is it made of gold, or is it just imitation? I always think that decorations that gentlemen wear are such gilded sepulchres. Your poor dear uncle John, who was run over by an omnibus, had a decoration from the Shah of Persia; it was just paste, my dear, paste."

"Mother," said Marjorie, who was unpinning the medal from her gown, "I am going to be married."

Mrs Stedman looked at her in amazement.

"Going to be married, Marjorie?" she said in a complaining voice. "My dear, you haven't told me anything about this, you know. A girl's best friend is her mother, and she should be the first to be told of anything of importance."

"I'm going to be married to Pretoria Smith," said the girl recklessly. "His name isn't Smith and he's nobody! He's a bushranger or a thief or a road agent or a bank robber or something, he's very rich – and he gets drunk!"

Mrs Stedman regarded her daughter with an alarmed eye.

"*You* haven't been drinking too much, dear, have you?" she asked. "It is awfully bad for young girls to drink. When I was young we had just one glass of port between three of us, and even that used to make my head go quite whizzy."

Marjorie had left the room and came back very shortly with her uncle's letter.

"I want you to read that, mother," she said. Mrs Stedman looked at her daughter suspiciously and fumbled for her glasses.

"Are you going to marry Lance?" she asked.

"Lance!" burst forth the girl, in such a tone of scorn that her mother shrank back open-mouthed.

"But he's a very nice boy, a dear boy," she insisted.

"Read that letter, mother," said the girl. "I shall go mad if you say much more to me."

Mrs Stedman fixed her glasses and read. When she had finished she was rather pale.

"Of course you're going to do it, darling, aren't you?" she said. "You don't know this gentleman, but I am perfectly sure your dear uncle would not recommend a husband unless he was quite a respectable person."

"So respectable that he came to the dinner tonight drunk, looking like a tramp," said the girl bitterly. "He insulted the Prince and collapsed over the table! And that brute Lance brought him in!"

"Lance would never do anything ungentlemanly, I'm sure," said Mrs Stedman. "But, my dear, you are going to marry him, aren't you?"

"I suppose so," said the girl.

"That's all right," said Mrs Stedman complacently, folding her glasses and putting them away. "It may turn out quite well for you. These romantic marriages sometimes do."

"Romantic! "repeated Marjorie in despair. "Mother, don't you realize what such a marriage to me means? Do you imagine that I, who must suffer, am going light-heartedly into this awful arrangement because I think it is romantic or hope that anything will come out of it but unhappiness?"

"Then, my dear," whimpered Mrs Stedman, "why do you go into it at all? I don't mind being turned out," she sniffed. "I don't mind starving and going into the bankruptcy court. If you feel so bitter about it, don't do it. Never mind me; I'm nobody." And she clucked spasmodically into her handkerchief.

Happily there was a knock at the door at that moment. The girl heard it, and Mrs Stedman heard it and forgot to grieve.

"I wonder who it is at this hour?" she said.

The girl had a horrible fear that it was Pretoria Smith, and it required all her efforts to stand still, and when the maid came in and announced Lance Kelman she was almost relieved.

"A MARRIAGE HAS BEEN ARRANGED – "

Mr Kelman was in a perturbed condition of mind. He had also had time to develop a grievance.

"Look here, Marjorie," he said, "I've been treated most shamefully by that infernal duke. I never did believe in royalties, anyway, and he – "

The girl stopped him with a gesture.

"Lance," she said quietly, "you behaved like a blackguard tonight. For what reason I cannot tell, except that your own miserable little vanity was hurt when you learnt I was going to marry – somebody else. Now don't interrupt me," she said, her voice rising. "You humiliated me before the whole of the county, because you thought that by so doing I would be disgusted with Pretoria Smith and marry you. I tell you this, Lance" – her shining eyes were fixed on his, and he quailed before them – "that I would sooner marry Pretoria Smith, or twenty Pretoria Smiths, than be married to a man like you. He may be a person of no education and know no better. You are a public school man and have the reputation of being a gentleman. To appease your miserable vanity you have made me the laughing-stock of Droitshire. You have deserved every word that the Prince said to you – and now, get out!"

She pointed to the door, and Lance Kelman, after a few ineffectual attempts to speak, slunk out, and had not thought of what he ought to have said under the circumstances till he was home in bed.

It was a restless night for Marjorie Stedman. Sleep would not come, and the dawn found her sitting in her silk kimono at the window, watching the stars fade in the western sky. The air was balmy, and the heavy scent of flowers came up to her. She did not feel in the least tired. The calm of the dawn hour brought comfort and peace to her troubled spirit.

Her room overlooked the road, for one end of the Priory was separated only by a dozen yards from the high screening hedge which divided the public thoroughfare from her mother's desmesne. The window afforded a view of that part of the road which led up from Tynewood, and presently she saw a man walking along in the middle of the road, coming toward her. She wondered if it were a labourer thus early afoot on his way to one of the farms, but somehow or other, from his walk, the easy swing of his stride, the almost cat-like lightness of tread, knew that he was no farmer's man. She sat watching until he came near at hand. He carried his hat in hand and his head was bare. And then with a gasp she recognized him. It was the man who had staggered into the hall the night before – Pretoria Smith. He was sober now, and possibly, she thought, he was walking off the effects of his night's debauch.

He looked neither to the right nor to the left, and only when he came abreast of her did he raise his eyes. She had intended to go back from the window so that he should not see her, but that quick uplift of his gaze had caught her by surprise. It surprised him too, apparently, for he stopped awkwardly and said something. She heard the word "Sorry," then jumped up and shut the casement window with a bang.

She did not even trouble to see what happened to him. If she had, she would have seen him turn with a shrug and continue his walk. Then, as she realized the futility of it all, she lay down on the bed, her head on her arms, too prostrate in spirit to weep. This man was to be her husband, and it was madness to start off as she was doing, to antagonize him from the start.

Her husband! She shuddered and, feeling cold, pulled the eiderdown over her. So lying she fell asleep and did not wake until ten o'clock. She had her bath, dressed slowly and came downstairs.

Mrs Stedman was in the drawing-room, a book in her hand, a cigarette between her lips. It was only since her acquaintance with Lady Tynewood that she had adopted this dashing practice, and Marjorie, despite her weariness of heart, was secretly amused, for her mother only smoked when she had some disagreeable office to perform.

"You're up, my dear?" said Mrs Stedman unnecessarily. "There are some letters for you."

The girl glanced at them and pushed them aside.

"You haven't had breakfast?"

"I've had some coffee in my room," said Marjorie shortly. Then, knowing the signs, she asked quietly: "Well, mother, what is the trouble?"

"My dear," said Mrs Stedman nervously, "I've had a letter from Alma – quite a nice letter, but – er – er – "

"But she wants her money, eh?" asked Marjorie.

Everything was conspiring against her – everything – everything. If she had wanted to change her mind, if, after the awful scene of the previous night, she had decided that under no circumstances could she marry this boor, the fates were deciding otherwise.

"She wants the money – yes," said Mrs Stedman apologetically. "Of course, Alma has very heavy expenses, my dear, and just now there's an unexpected call upon her. I'll read you her letter if you like."

"You needn't trouble, mother. I know all about the unexpected calls that Lady Tynewood has upon her slender resources," said the girl. "You mustn't forget that I've been writing to thousands of people for money, in connection with the hospital, and I know just what they say in certain circumstances."

"Alma was very generous to your fund," said Mrs Stedman reproachfully. "Very generous indeed, I thought."

"She gave a hundred pounds, and expected a thousand pounds' worth of advertisement," said the girl curtly. "And she'd very gladly take back her hundred pounds if she could get it. So she wants the money, does she? By when?"

"By next Monday. It is very dreadful that I should have to beg my own daughter to help me in this matter," said Mrs Stedman tearfully. "I thought I could arrange without asking you to help me, for my luck yesterday was extraordinarily good."

"You played again?" asked the girl quickly. "Oh, mother, mother!"

"Why shouldn't I?" demanded Mrs Stedman, bridling. "Gracious heavens, girl! One would think that I was not capable of looking after myself."

Marjorie sighed, and walking to the window, opened it on to the lawn. She stood there contemplating the garden for a while, and then turned back to the other.

"Mother," she said, "how quickly can I be married?"

"How quickly?" repeated Mrs Stedman. "I don't know how long it takes a dressmaker to prepare – "

"I'm not thinking about dressmakers," said Marjorie quietly. "I'm thinking about marriage. How long notice does one have to give before the actual ceremony can be performed?"

"Of course, if you get a special licence – though I don't believe in these hurried weddings," said her mother – "it can be done in a day or two."

"Hurried!" Marjorie laughed. "Oh yes, it'll be hurried all right. I wish you would telephone Mr Curtis to fix this licence," she said, referring to the lawyer of the village. And her mother looked uncomfortable.

"You don't owe Mr Curtis money too, do you?" she asked quickly.

"Well, my dear," faltered Mrs Stedman, "there's the interest on the mortgage. I think I told you that the house was mortgaged."

"It hasn't been paid, I suppose." Marjorie shook her head.

"Of course I can arrange it," said Mrs Stedman with dignity. "I will speak to Mr Curtis and explain to him just what I want."

She walked to her writing desk and took a sheet of paper. Presently:

"Marjorie Mary Stedman" she repeated as she wrote, "daughter of Maud Stedman and John Francis Stedman, gentleman." She wrote a little more and then turned. "What is your fiancé's name, dear?" she asked, in the most natural manner, as though it were the most usual, instead of being the most fantastic marriage that had ever been arranged.

"My fiancé's name?" said Marjorie, and then with a gasp: "I — I don't know his name!"

.

LADY TYNEWOOD MAKES A CALL

Lady Tynewood came down to her panelled dining-room and disturbed Mr Augustus Javot in his study of the day's racing. He was the same tall lank man, upon whom the passing of time worked no apparent change. Though his name was French, he came of an old English family in the north, though very few members of that family boasted of the fact. He was supposed to be secretary, factotum and bailiff to Lady Tynewood, but his attitude to her was not that of the hired servant.

She swept into the room, and even in the cruel light of morning her unlined face was pleasant to look upon.

"Javot," she said.

He did not look up.

"Javot," she said more sharply, and he turned his face to hers with a sigh of patient resignation.

"Why do you interrupt me?" he grumbled. "You know I hate it when I am reading the sporting news."

She had taken a little cigarette from a jewelled case and had lit it.

"Javot, do you remember all I told you last night about what happened at the County Hall?"

"I remember," he said. "There was a row or something, wasn't there? This South African gentleman intruded himself and was chucked out."

"He was gracefully escorted from the room by a prince of the blood," said the woman sardonically. "It was Lance Kelman who was chucked out."

"He's a fool," growled the other.

"But a useful fool," said Alma, Lady Tynewood, quietly. "He's half in love with that girl and a little judicious prompting will make him wholly in love. I hate her," she said viciously.

Javot leaned back in his chair, thrust his hands deep into his breeches pockets, and smiled.

"A pretty girl," he said thoughtfully, "a very pretty girl indeed. I remember – " he stopped himself. Mr Javot was not communicative even to Lady Tynewood. He had recognized the girl the first time he had seen her and had been surprised that she had not recalled his face. "And she's going to marry this – er – miner, eh?" he went on. "One of nature's noblemen, or just an ordinary rough diamond that wants a bit of polishing?"

She sat on the edge of the table, swinging her legs and puffing little rings of smoke into the clear air.

"I went to Tynewood Chase yesterday," she said, "and they wouldn't let me in."

"You're a fool to go to Tynewood Chase," said the man coolly. "I've told you a dozen times not to do it. Why aren't you content to sit and wait? Sooner or later Tynewood will die and the whole of that property will pass into your possession. Including the famous Tynewood collar," he added significantly.

She did not make any answer to this, being still engaged in the pursuit of her thoughts.

"I want to see this Pretoria Smith," she said. "He is one of those wandering creatures who might have come against James. A strong, powerful face," she mused. "I am not so sure – " She stopped herself in time.

"What aren't you so sure about?" he asked suspiciously.

"Nothing," she replied with a light toss of her head. "But he might give us information, don't you think?"

"It's unlikely," said Javot. "Let James Tynewood alone, I tell you, and sit tight. You've got a fine income from the estate; you're young enough to be able to afford to wait a year or two. You're not pretending," he said sarcastically, "that you are worrying your head about him, whether he is alive or dead – you're not putting over that madly-in-love stuff, are you? You only knew him for a few weeks and he was drunk when he married you."

"You're crude, Javot." She jumped down from the table and threw away her cigarette, but there was no resentment in her voice. "Just brutally crude, Javot. Of course he was drunk when he married me, otherwise he would never have made such a fool of himself. If you hadn't kept him up all night playing cards, dosing him with absinthe and brandy, and if you hadn't brought him, in a condition near to madness, to the registrar's office in the Marylebone Road, I should not have married him, and you and I would not have been sitting here living in comfort at Monk House."

He scratched his chin.

"I suppose you're right," he admitted. "But isn't that my argument? Leave well alone."

"Not when there's better," she replied. "I want proof of James Tynewood's death. You and I have been brought up in a hard school, Javot. We know how long that kind of man lasts who drinks and plays the fool game as that boy did. A hot climate would finish him off."

"If we'd only had a photograph of him to circulate, we might have got news," said Javot thoughtfully. "But he never seems to have had a picture taken. I've tried every big photographer's in London to get a picture of James Tynewood and had the same story throughout."

"And yet he ought not to be difficult to find," persisted the woman. "He had lost the little finger of his left hand, you remember."

Javot nodded.

"He had it blown off by a gun when he was a boy."

Mr Javot had settled himself down again to his paper and only grunted a reply. She looked at him and laughed.

"I am going out," she said.

"Where are you going?" he asked.

"I'm going over to see dear Maud Stedman," she mimicked.

"What about that money?"

"I've written to her for it – told her I had heavy liabilities to meet."

"Can she pay, do you think?" asked Javot, who always took an interest in matters of finance.

"She'll pay all right. This daughter of hers is going to marry a rich man – Lance told me all about it last night. I was a fool to have written for the money under the circumstances, but the letter was posted before Lance took me into his confidence. I mustn't create a bad impression, so I'm going over to tell her that the money can stand over for a hundred years or so." She laughed, and Mr Javot's approving grin was her reward.

Mrs Stedman was on the lawn, feeding the birds, when Lady Tynewood came swinging up the drive in a chic walking costume, twirling her stick as she came. She kissed the visitor affectionately.

"Oh, Alma, dear," she said nervously, "about that money – "

"My dear, sweet woman," said Alma with her sweetest smile, "you're not to talk about the money again. I have managed to meet all my bills without troubling my friends, so you can consider my letter as not having been written. Now give me a nice cup of tea. I love it in the morning."

Mrs Stedman made a mysterious sign and glanced at the house.

"My dear," she said, dropping her voice, though there was no need to, for she was fully fifty yards from the nearest window, "we cannot go into the house. He – he is there."

"He?" repeated Alma, mystified. "Which particular 'he' are you talking about?"

"My daughter's fiancé," said Mrs Stedman primly. "Mr – er – Mr Pretoria."

"He's the man I'm dying to see," said Alma, and made her way across the lawn.

THE MEETING

He had come. Marjorie had not expected that he would so soon after his disgraceful exhibition of the previous night. But apparently he had no shame. She had watched her mother go out of the room and had settled to write a letter of thanks to Lord Wadham, when there came a tap on the door and a maid, a little agitated as though she knew some of the precious secrets of the house – as probably she did – came in.

"Mr Pretoria Smith," she said breathlessly. Then the man came in, and Marjorie rose to meet him.

They stood facing one another for the space of two seconds. He saw a girl of delicate beauty, and the sight of her took his breath away. It is true that he had not seen her on the previous night, and had only glimpsed her in the morning, guessing who she was. But now the revelation of her exquisite sweetness came like a blow to him.

She, for her part, saw a tall man, not so broad of shoulder as she had imagined he was. His face was tanned brown by the African sun, his eyes were a deep blue (and bloodshot, she noticed, and guessed the cause). It was a mask-like face, designed to hide whatever passions he felt, and in repose was just a little forbidding. He was still dressed in the shabby suit he had worn on the previous night. It hung loosely on him, as though it had been made for a larger and shorter man.

It was a terribly awkward moment for both of them.

"I'm the man your uncle wrote about," he said jerkily. "I am called Pretoria Smith, but that – that isn't my name."

She never imagined it was his name, but made no comment. Not even when he added: "I wish to be married in that name. It makes no difference to the legality of the marriage – I might get into trouble, but the marriage would be legal," he ended lamely.

To her the matter of names seemed so small and unimportant compared with the big fact that she had to marry at all.

"I need not introduce myself," she said quietly. "I am Marjorie Stedman, Solomon Stedman's niece. I have seen you before – in Mr Vance's office. I was his secretary."

He stared at her.

"In Vance's office?" he said. "Lord, I remember!"

He frowned a little as though trying to recall her face and she prayed that he might not associate her with that terrible night at Tynewood Chase. Apparently he did not.

"Won't you sit down?" she said, and he seated himself, ill at ease, on the edge of an armchair. And this she noticed, that he kept his eyes upon her steadily, unwaveringly. It might have embarrassed her but for the fact that she preferred that to the shiftless look she expected.

"You are a friend of my uncle's?" she asked, by way of making polite conversation.

"A very dear friend," he said, clearing his throat. "We have known each other for – four years. I saved his life," he said gauchely.

"Indeed?" she asked, with that same polite interest in her voice.

"He was out prospecting," said the man. "He had just located the Kalahari Reef, which made his fortune and mine, when he lost track of the waterhole. The two boys – natives, you know, we call them boys there, whatever their ages are – led them astray. I think they wanted to see him dead so that they could take his belongings. I happened along at the moment when he was near to death, within a yard or two of the waterhole, but too weak to reach it."

"And you gave him water?" she asked, and tried to visualize that scene in the desert.

"Yes," he hesitated. "I made them give him water, and then I took him back to the nearest township."

"And the 'boys'?" she asked.

He looked around the room.

"Oh, I shot one eventually. He gave trouble," he said, and she shuddered. "I think I killed him; I am not certain. The other one was useful, and he didn't show fight, of course."

There followed another long pause, and it was Marjorie Stedman who again broke the silence.

"Mr Smith," she said quietly, "my uncle wishes me to marry you, and I think you have been − persuaded " − she flushed as she used the hateful word − "to agree."

He nodded.

"I didn't wish to − naturally," he said. "And now least of all. I owe Solomon a lot, and his heart is set upon this. He is a crazy old devil," he said, half to himself, but there was affection in his tone, and the girl found herself nearly smiling.

"Why did you want persuading?" she asked.

"Because," he hesitated, "well, because I didn't want to marry any woman, and certainly not a woman I did not know. That was one reason," he said, "the other was the woman herself. I realized what a terrible thing it must be for a girl to have some man thrown at her head."

She looked at him a little wonderingly and he, misunderstanding the reason, flushed a little.

"I must apologize for this clothing," he said. "I bought it at a store in a hurry, and I only caught the boat by the skin of my teeth and came straight here. And I want very badly to apologize, Miss Stedman," he said earnestly, "for last night."

"I don't think we'll talk about that," she said gently. "But I do hope that when" − she could not say the words for a while − "when we are married you will not − drink."

He made no reply to this, and at that moment Lady Tynewood came through the French windows.

"Now, my dear," she said gaily, addressing the girl, murder in her eyes, "introduce me to your fiancé."

Pretoria Smith turned slowly and his hand was outstretched as the girl said, with a miserable attempt at gaiety:

"I want you to meet Mr Smith, Lady Tynewood."

For a second they stood face to face, the woman looking upon the tall figure with some admiration. And then Marjorie saw a look of malignity, a look of horror, come into the man's face, and he took a step back, raising his hand as though to ward off the smiling Alma.

"You – you!" His voice was hoarse and passionate. "My God! I would sooner shake hands with a leper!"

A MARRIAGE WAS ARRANGED

For a moment he stared, and Lady Tynewood, shrinking back before the vengeful hatred in this stranger's face, saw his eyes narrow. And then Pretoria Smith snatched up his hat from the chair, pushed past her, and walked rapidly across the lawn.

They looked at one another, speechless with amazement. Marjorie, pale as death, could do no more than stare after the figure with wide-open eyes. Lady Tynewood was the first to recover.

"So that is your lover?" she said dryly. "A perfect type of gentleman. I congratulate you."

Marjorie did not reply. Her mother had come in behind Alma, and had been a fluttered and agitated spectator of the scene.

"He was very rude," she said feebly.

At first Lady Tynewood had been amused, but now she was angry.

"Did you put him up to that?" she asked, trembling with passion. "Or is that a specimen of his natural colonial manners?"

The girl was experiencing an extraordinary sensation. She was called upon to defend a man the very mention of whose name was hateful.

"Mr Smith must have very excellent reasons," she said slowly. "I thought for one happy moment that it was your long-lost husband returning, Lady Tynewood."

She was being unpardonably rude; more – she was being wicked and cruel. She was talking flippantly of the dead, as she knew, but she did not care.

"My husband!" scoffed Alma. "My husband was a gentleman – is a gentleman," she corrected. "A little bit of a thing like you," she said contemptuously, "without half this man's nerve – " She bent her brows in an effort of memory. She seemed oblivious of the company. "I can't place him," she said, speaking her thoughts aloud. "I wonder where I've met him."

She looked at the girl with a speculative eye.

"My dear, you're going to have a happy married life, I don't think!" she said, as she went from the room.

Marjorie hardly heard her. Not waiting for lunch, she ordered her horse to be brought round and rode over to Lord Wadham's big house. She knew that the Prince had left in the early morning and that the Earl would be visible. She found him walking in the park and overtook him on the main drive.

"Hello!" roared Lord Wadham. "What the devil do you want so early in the morning?"

"I'm going to be married," she blurted, "to – to rather an awful person."

"The devil, you are!" For once Lord Wadham's voice was quiet and then suddenly he slapped his leg. "I've got it," he said. "The lad who was full of wine last night!" And she flushed.

"Yes," she said in a low voice, "that is my fiancé."

"Johannesburg Jones or something, or Maritzburg Mike."

"Pretoria Smith," she said.

"Gad! You don't say so? What on earth makes you marry a gentleman of that calibre?" he asked seriously. "I didn't have a good look at his face, but I'll bet he's a wrong 'un. A man who would wear a ready-made suit of clothes would commit a murder."

She laughed.

"You mustn't judge him harshly," she said. "There – there may be explanations." Then: "Lord Wadham," she asked breathlessly, "I wonder if you could do something for me?"

"I'll do anything in the world for you, my dear," said the Earl kindly. "If I hadn't a wife and four children I'd marry you like a shot. But her ladyship – God bless her! – is hale and hearty. She's one of the Wingleys of Norfolk, and may live to ninety," he added good-humouredly.

"It is something to do with marriage that I wanted to ask your advice about," she said with a smile.

"You want to be married at once, eh?" he said thoughtfully, when she had finished telling him. "I can manage that for you. But, my dear, aren't you taking too great a risk? Even for the sake of – " He hesitated. He had heard stories of the inefficient Mrs Stedman, and knew something, much more than the girl could guess, about this new passion for gambling. "Even for the sake of those you love," he said bluntly. "There, there, my dear, I didn't mean to make you feel uncomfortable. Yours is a terrible situation and I would do anything to help you. What is the man like?"

She smiled a little glumly.

"He's like – Pretoria Smith," she said, as lightly as she could.

Lord Wadham was rubbing his chin.

"I can fix the marriage certificate. Let me have the names."

She could not tell him that she was ignorant of her husband's name.

"I will send them," she said.

(In sheer desperation when she got back she sat down at her desk and wrote blindly: "John Smith, son of Henry and Mary Smith," and described Henry Smith at random as a "miner" and gave the date of his birth as thirty-two years before.)

"I will fix this up for you right away," he said. "And if you let me have the names today I will send you the licence by the first post tomorrow."

"Where could I be married?" she asked.

"Oh, almost anywhere," he said. "My chaplain will come over and marry you with pleasure. You don't know Stoneham, do you? He's an excellent fellow – an Oxford blue, as blind as a bat and nearly as deaf as an owl."

He chuckled with joy at his description of the unfortunate clergyman.

"The very fellow for you, my dear," he said. "He'd never know you again and wouldn't recognize your husband if he wore bells in his ears.

But where? Humph!" He considered again. "I have it," he said, slapping his hands together. "I'll wire to a friend of mine who's one of the Tynewood trustees and ask permission for you to be married in the private chapel of Tynewood Chase. Vance, the lawyer."

"Mr Vance!" she repeated in astonishment. "Why, of course! But do you think he will – he – he is very particular about people even going over the place."

"I'll fix it, my dear," said Lord Wadham confidently. "Now how would it be if I arranged about the chapel, sent Stoneham over, came along and gave you away myself?"

Tears filled the girl's eyes.

"You are more than kind to me, Lord Wadham," she said tremulously.

He patted her shoulder in his kind way.

"Nonsense!" he said. "I love marrying people off, though I can't say that I'm very much in love with this marriage. Will you agree, if I can fix the chapel and the parson?"

She nodded.

"And what date?" he asked.

"I – I will see Mr Smith," she said.

She met Pretoria Smith that afternoon, though she had no idea that she would see him. She had sent a note down to the one inn which the village boasted, asking him to come and see her, but evidently this did not reach him. She was taking a walk in the afternoon, and had covered two quick miles across the rolling downs, when, coming to a turn in the highway, where the road dipped down into the valley, she saw a man sitting on the grass, his hands clasping his chin, his head bent forward till his chin touched his knees. At the sound of her footsteps he looked round. It was Pretoria Smith and he jumped to his feet.

"I'm very sorry about this morning," he said with a certain gruffness. "I was a fool to lose my temper with that – with the lady."

"You know Lady Tynewood?" asked the girl.

"Know her?" he said bitterly. "Yes, I know the lady!"

"She's the wife of Sir James Tynewood, you know, who is a big landowner in these parts, though he has never lived here."

She watched him as she spoke. How would he take the reference to the man who had died so tragically that night years ago? He did not so much as wince.

"Doesn't live here? Then he's a fool," said Pretoria Smith brusquely, "for this is the most beautiful country I've seen. Perhaps it is after the wide spaces and the dry and arid character of a South African landscape that this is so especially enchanting," he said, "but you can take it from me that Sir James is a fool."

"Mr Smith," – she hated saying what she had to say, – "I was going to ask you this morning if you would object to our – our marriage taking place very quickly?"

"The sooner the better," said he. He had turned his face from her and was looking across the valley.

"You see," she went on, playing with a bangle and not raising her eyes, "it is all so unexpected and – and shocking for me. When I say shocking," she added quickly, "I do not mean to use that word in the usual sense of the term."

"I dare say you do, really," he replied, "and I think you're quite right. I've been rather shocked too. I think I explained to you that I had no more idea of getting married than the man in the moon. I wanted to be left alone quietly on the mine with my pipe and my thoughts, which weren't always pleasant, but were comparatively cheerful, compared with the state of my mind at this moment."

She shot a quick glance at him.

"That isn't very complimentary, you know," she said with a little laugh. "But I don't expect compliments. Do you mind getting married almost at once?"

"You want to get it over," said the other, nodding at a cow that was browsing down the slope of the hill. "I don't blame you. I feel a little that way myself, and it cannot be too soon."

"Lord Wadham suggests that I should be married by his chaplain," she said. "Will that suit you?"

"Stoneham?" he asked carelessly. "He used to be vicar here – he's nearly blind."

"Do you know him?" she asked quickly.

He coloured under the tan.

"I have been listening to village gossip," he confessed. "No, I don't know Lord Wadham or his chaplain, but it seems to me that one chaplain is very much like another."

"And – and I've given your name as John Smith. Is it John?"

"Very nearly," he replied. "You can call me anything you like. Have you described my illustrious ancestors?"

"I did make an attempt," she confessed. "I said your father was a miner."

He laughed softly.

"That's right," he said. "He dug up things – mostly weeds on the garden path; he was rather fanatical about weeds, and the gardeners lived in terror of him."

"And – and" she went on – she wanted to get this out and done with – "Lord Wadham suggested that, as I do not want a great deal of publicity, or you either, I suppose " – he shook his head – "we could be married very quietly in the chapel at Tynewood Chase."

He did not reply.

"Is there a chapel in Tynewood Chase?" he said after a very long interval of silence. She rather despised him for that piece of pretence.

"Yes," she nodded, "a very pretty chapel. I thought of seeing it today. Wouldn't you – wouldn't you like to come?"

He shook his head.

"Not very much," he confessed, and somehow she expected that answer.

"So it is all right?" she asked. "And what day?"

"Any time." He was still looking away.

"Then I may regard it as settled." She made a move as though to go on. "Shall I say at eleven o'clock?"

"An excellent hour," said he.

"And – and" – she swallowed something – "where shall we go afterwards?"

IN THE LANE

He was on his feet now and he turned round.

"I'm sorry," he said, and his voice was gentle. "I'm afraid you think I'm rather a boor, and I am being one really. I've been so long away with those thoughts of mine, Miss Stedman, that I've forgotten how to think, as well as how to talk, in a civilized fashion. Your arrangements will do splendidly."

She raised her eyes to his and saw in them a kindness that she had never suspected.

"And afterwards I will arrange for a car."

He looked round at his shabby clothes.

"I have nothing better than these, but I have ordered some clothes from London. What is your name – Marjorie, isn't it?" he asked.

"Yes."

"Marjorie." He repeated the name softly. "I shall have to call you Marjorie. I hope you won't mind."

She laughed in spite of herself.

"I believe it is customary amongst married people to call one another by their Christian names," she said.

She had a feeling that there was something he wanted to say and lingered. But he did not speak until she definitely bade him goodbye.

"I'll walk a little way with you," he said. "Are you going back?"

She nodded. It was a queer sensation walking with him. He was a head taller than she, she noted. She had always liked tall men, but she was not prepared to extend her liking to Pretoria Smith.

"It sounded ungallant to you when I told you that I had come against my will to marry you," he said unexpectedly. "But it was no more than the truth. I owe Solomon so much that I couldn't refuse him; and even if I made the offer which is in my heart, I know I should still be going back on him and double-crossing him."

"The offer?" she asked in surprise. "What offer?"

"My offer is a very simple one," he said quietly. "I realize you are marrying me because you cannot afford to lose Solomon's income. I only learnt of that threat he made to you just before I sailed. Solomon's heart is fixed upon this marriage. He is scared to death lest his money falls into the hands of" – he nearly said 'Lance Kelman' but changed the words to 'a man who will marry you because you are wealthy.' "Really, Miss Stedman, I want you to believe that Solomon's first idea is your happiness. He has spoken to me about you so often. He used to love the letters you sent to him when you were a child, and has kept every one of them."

The girl was touched, and tears rose to her eyes.

"Poor uncle!" she said softly. "I'm sure he's doing what he thinks is best."

"Bear that in mind," Pretoria Smith went on, "and you will understand my dilemma. I would willingly give you a quarter of a million pounds to enable you to decline me, with or without thanks," he added with a little smile that illuminated his face and made him look ten years younger.

She had stopped and was looking at him in amazement.

"I couldn't do that," she said. "I have given my word to uncle. I telegraphed to him the day I received his letter."

"I was afraid you would," he said gloomily. "But I was afraid too that if I made the offer you would accept. And that would have been unfair on Solomon. It wasn't a question of money that distressed him, it was a question of your safety from the fortune-hunter. And if I'd made you a rich woman, as I could, for I am as well off as Solomon – in fact, infinitely better off," he smiled again – "you would have been exposed to the same danger, though that danger may have been a very slight one."

They had resumed their walk and she was pacing slowly by his side, when they heard the clatter of two horses and drew closer into the hedge to allow the riders to pass.

They were Lance Kelman and Lady Tynewood, and at the sight of these two Kelman's face went dark. Well, indeed, had Alma played upon his feelings, for he who had before only taken a dilettante interest in his cousin, now regarded her as the love of his life and himself as the most injured of men.

He did not pass but put his horse squarely in their path, and Alma watched the scene with malicious amusement.

"So you've got your Pretoria Smith, have you, Marjorie?" cried Kelman loudly. He had lunched very well with Lady Tynewood, and much golden wine had flowed.

Marjorie, pink of face, eyed him steadily, but did not reply.

"I suppose, by this time, you're in love with this fellow?" said Lance Kelman with a raucous laugh. "He's got the money, hasn't he? And the dear old lady is in debt. Well, you're welcome to the drunken brute. You saw what kind of man he was last night when I brought him in – "

In two strides Pretoria Smith was at his side, his hand resting on the knee of the horseman.

"You brought him in?" he said softly. "I have heard this morning something of my behaviour last night, of which I have no particular memory. Were you the gentleman that introduced me to that company?"

"Take your hand off me, you swine!" roared Kelman, and struck at Pretoria Smith with his whip.

Marjorie screamed and shrank back, but the whip never touched the man. Instead, Lance Kelman's wrist was caught in a grip of steel.

"There are certain things you must not do," said Pretoria Smith as softly as before. "Can you swim?"

"Let go!" yelled Lance, struggling to free himself.

"Can you swim?" asked the other again. And then, before Kelman could answer, he was jerked violently from his horse.

For a moment he was poised in the air above Pretoria Smith, and then he hurtled like a stone into a large green-covered pond that flanked the road at this point. He fell with a splutter and a yell but rose immediately a somewhat ludicrous object.

"I'll pay you for this, you nigger-murdering dog! Tell her about the men you've flogged and the niggers you've killed!"

The face of Pretoria Smith was deadly white, and his voice shook.

"I'm sorry I lost my temper," he said in a low voice as Mr Kelman waded painfully ashore. He did not look up at the woman on the horse. "You are in bad company, my friend."

"I should imagine you are an authority on the subject of bad company."

It was Lady Tynewood who spoke and then he raised his eyes to her face.

"At least I never attended one of your parties, Miss Trebizond," he said, using her stage name.

The woman tried to smile and then her wandering eyes met Marjorie's and she started. For she recognized in this radiant girl the little typist who had come to her flat the night of her marriage.

THE WEDDING

"It is all mysterious and strange and rather terrible," thought Marjorie, as she sat in the tiny Norman chapel of Tynewood Chase, waiting for the arrival of her future husband. She was thinking of Alma and Sir James Tynewood and of Pretoria Smith. But mostly she was thinking of the latter.

The clergyman had come, and was all that Lord Wadham had described him. A quiet, scholarly man, near-sighted and a little deaf, he too was waiting in the miniature vestry, and Lord Wadham was with him.

Pretoria Smith seemed less terrible to her now, this strange man from the south. She had not seen him since that day they parted on the road, leaving behind them a bedraggled Lance Kelman.

It was her wedding day! She could not believe it. The unreality of it was terrible. It was almost laughable. Her mother had wanted to accompany her, but her mother would have been the last straw, and she had been persuaded to remain behind.

One of the caretakers of the Chase was showing her round the chapel. The walls were covered with memorial tablets, and in the six alcoves beneath windows of beautiful design and colour were the tombs of the ancient Tynewoods. She was really impressed, though she thought she could not have imagined a queerer way of spending her wedding morning than by examining the tombs of the dead, even the illustrious dead.

Suddenly she stopped before a tomb, and as she read the name she reeled.

NORMAN GARRICK

That was all. No date, no other particular. Norman Garrick! The lawyer had told her that was the real name of Pretoria Smith. She knew it was a lie, but for the first time she realized the extent of his deception. Why had the lawyer deceived her, he the kindliest and most truthful of men? Her guide did not seem to notice her perturbation and she followed him dazed and stunned.

He showed her the ancient arms carved on one of the pillars by a Tynewood to whom the chapel was a prison in the days of King Charles, and who had only emerged to his execution.

"They're a queer lot, the Tynewoods, miss," explained the servitor. "I don't know the last gentleman, Sir James, but I dare say he's like the rest of them."

Lord Wadham had come from the vestry and the clergyman in his robes had followed. She turned to the Earl with relief. She must think of tangible, real things or she would go mad.

"Isn't it time he was here?" asked his lordship, looking at his watch impatiently. "You've got a very dilatory bridegroom, my dear. He's ten minutes late."

A quarter of an hour passed, twenty minutes and half an hour, and still he did not come, and Lord Wadham was growing apoplectic when there was a sound of unsteady footsteps in the hall, and Pretoria Smith staggered in and stood one moment to steady himself, his hand against a stone pillar. He was unkempt, unshaven, wild of eye and they saw that he was holding himself up with an effort. Then slowly he walked down the aisle and took his place by the side of the affrighted girl. She scarcely dared breathe.

"Drunk, by heaven!" murmured Lord Wadham, and looked at the clergyman.

But the clergyman saw nothing and heard little. He had opened his book at the proper place, and now the ceremony was proceeding, and all the time the man at her side was swaying to the left and to the right. That ceremony was a dream, a bad dream, but presently she heard the clergyman's voice, like one that came from far away:

"…let no man put asunder."

And she knew that for good or ill she was this man's wife, Mrs Pretoria Smith – Mrs Nobody, the wife of a man who claimed the name of one whose mouldering dust was almost under her feet!

The clergyman raised his hand in benediction and Pretoria Smith stumbled on to his knees, and his head was bowed.

It was over at last. Wadham touched Pretoria Smith on the shoulder.

"Come on, get up, man," he said, but Pretoria Smith rolled over on his side, and when Wadham bent down he found him fast asleep.

There was a long and painful silence, which Lord Wadham interrupted.

"I will get the car, my dear," he said in a low voice, and she saw that he was genuinely distressed and put out her hand to him.

"The car is waiting outside," she said in a stifled voice. "Perhaps the journey will – help him." But she choked a sob in her throat.

"Where are you going?" he asked.

"To Brightsea," she said. "To a cottage on the common, far away from – the town, thank heaven! Do you think we could get him into the car?"

With the assistance of the caretaker, the chauffeur, who was brought in for the purpose, and Lord Wadham, the sleeping man was wakened and supported to the limousine and pushed into a corner.

"I think you'd better have the car closed," said Lord Wadham, and the girl assented silently.

In her eyes was all the tragedy of all the women in the world as she turned to thank the Earl.

"Goodbye and good luck!" he said. "I hate to see you go like this, but God knows I cannot stop you."

She did not speak but entered the limousine, and the chauffeur slammed the door behind her.

Thus did Marjorie Smith go forth upon her honeymoon.

LADY TYNEWOOD HAS AN IDEA

Lord Wadham watched the car disappear with a look of sorrow. Then, dropping a tip into the attendant's hand, he had walked slowly down the drive and through the iron gates. He knew the wooden-faced old man at the gates, and replied to his salute.

"Well, Hill, any news of your master?"

"No, my lord," said the man stolidly. "But he'll come back one of these days."

"A very sad affair, Hill," boomed Lord Wadham.

"Aye, my lord, it was a bad affair, and only them as knows the true story knows how bad it was."

"Do you know, Hill?"

"No, my lord," said the man, looking past his lordship.

"I believe you're an infernal old liar," said Lord Wadham good-naturedly, "but if you keep your master's secrets, my boy, you'll live to a ripe old age! I wish to heaven I had a few like you. By the way, what happened to the brother of Sir James?"

"The half-brother, you mean, my lord," said Hill.

"Yes, yes, he was the half-brother, of course. He was rather a nice boy, too."

"He died, my lord, some years ago," said Hill. "Died of fever – typhoid fever, that's the word."

"How long ago was that?"

"I can't tell you, my lord," said Hill. "It was some time when Sir James was in London – getting married. Maybe before or maybe after,

I can't quite recall the circumstance. Dr Fordham attended him – that was Sir James's great friend, who used to go abroad with him a lot."

"Fordham? Fordham?" said his lordship, knitting his brows. "I don't remember that doctor."

"He wasn't a native of these parts, my lord. I think he was an Irish gentleman. I hear he's dead too. He died of influenza or something of that sort."

Lord Wadham was rolling and unrolling his umbrella.

"Do you ever see Lady Tynewood here?" he asked, and the man smothered his smile.

"Yes, my lord," he said quietly. "My lady comes sometimes but we don't admit her."

"The order still stands, does it?" said Lord Wadham.

"Her ladyship's over there at this minute," said the gamekeeper, nodding. "She's been here ever since the wedding party went in, and has been there since the wedding party went out." He pointed to a side lane where a portion of the back and one wheel of Lady Tynewood's car was visible.

Lady Tynewood was a clever woman. She had an imagination which enabled her to anticipate happenings that an ordinary person would not have dreamt of. If Lord Wadham wondered why she had planted herself near the gates of Tynewood Chase, and, wondering, had come to the conclusion that she was merely a curious spectator of the wedding, he was altogether wrong. It was Lord Wadham himself who was the attraction, did he but know it. He was blessed with a stentorian voice, which carried far, as Lady Tynewood well knew.

She was also aware of the fact that Lord Wadham knew the oldest of the Tynewood servants, the man who kept the gate, and if there was a talk between the two, she would overhear the gist of it. It is true that she had made a discovery of greater importance than Lord Wadham's indiscretion could reveal, but that had been by accident. For the first time she had learnt of a brother. Who was this brother who had died?

And now she had a clue. The name of Dr Fordham had been used in connection with the brother's death, and Fordham was a friend of Sir James, and presumably a friend of the family.

Lord Wadham had to pass the end of the lane in order to reach his own machine, which was farther along the road. He was most anxious to avoid a meeting with Lady Tynewood; but Lady Tynewood was of another opinion, and planted herself in his way.

"Good morning, Lord Wadham," she said pleasantly, when he took off his hat.

"Good morning, Lady Tynewood," he answered, and added, not without malice: "Have you been to the wedding?"

She smiled.

"Unfortunately, I am not admitted into my own house," she said, "but I've seen the wedding party. Mr Pretoria Smith seemed a little – unwell, didn't he?"

"He has – er – been rather ill," said his lordship handsomely, "but I noticed nothing abnormal in his appearance."

The slow, cynical smile that dawned on her face irritated him, and with another flourish of his hat he was moving on, but again she stopped him.

"Lord Wadham, you're a friend of Miss Stedman's?"

"I am a friend of Mrs Smith's," he said pointedly.

"Call her what you like – I remember her best as a – a sort of messenger girl for a firm of lawyers in the city," she said with a careless shrug. "But as you are her friend, you will naturally be glad to see her released from that man, as very soon she shall be – and in a particularly disagreeable way," she said deliberately. "And if the servant's gossip I have heard can be crystallized into facts – "

The old peer smiled at her with his eyes.

"Marriages are somewhat difficult to dissolve," he said sweetly, "as your ladyship probably knows."

She stared after his retreating figure, then walked back to where the bored Mr Javot was sitting on a step of the car.

"I wonder what he meant by that?" she asked.

"What does anybody mean by anything?" said Javot irritably. "Are you going to keep me here all day?"

"Marriages are difficult to dissolve," she repeated.

"Well, ain't they?" asked Javot, and laughed loudly.

THE HONEYMOON

Marjorie kept her eyes straight ahead of her, sinking back into a corner of the car, not daring to look at the man she had married in such extraordinary circumstances. When they had passed the gates of the Chase and had reached the open country, she did look round. The man was asleep, breathing heavily. His fingers, which lay clasped lightly on his lap, were twitching.

"He may choke," she thought, for though his shirt was collarless except for the soft collar which was attached to it, it had been buttoned up to his neck.

She bent over and loosened the button with icy fingers and his breath came against her cheek. She looked at him in amazement. Once she had been kissed by a man in wine (the memory recalled Lady Tynewood and the parties she gave) and she had never forgotten the hated smell of that vinous breath. But there was no such scent here. She wondered what she could do. Perhaps he had some sobering agent in his possession; she had heard of such things. She hesitated, then began to search in his waistcoat pockets. In the first there was a watch which had stopped apparently the night before; in the upper waistcoat pocket was a small black case, and she took it out and opened the lid, almost recoiling in horror at the sight. It was a hypodermic syringe such as drug-takers use. So that was it! She looked at the thing; it was brand-new, and she recognized with a start of surprise the name on the silk lining of Tynewood's one chemist.

In the case were a number of small pellets in a microscopic glass case.

"Strychnine," she mused, and frowned. People do not take strychnine as a sedative or a narcotic.

She put the case into her bag and sat looking at him for some time. It made very little difference whether she was married to a drunkard or a drug-taker, she thought, with a shrug. She had a blank feeling of despair whenever she thought of the future, and the incidentals to her life were not really of any importance.

The car sped on over hill and down dale, across great plains, skirting the edge of shady forests, but the girl had no eyes for the beauty of the scene, no thought for the charm or perfection of the day, for the blue sky overhead or the gentle wind which brushed her cheeks.

The car pulled up by the side of a wild common, and the chauffeur got down.

"Did you bring any lunch, madam?" he asked, "or would you prefer that I should call at an inn? There's a town just ahead of us." He looked significantly at the slumbering figure.

"Thank you," said the girl. "I have a luncheon basket; you will find it strapped on the carrier."

"Excuse me asking, miss," said the chauffeur – it was Lord Wadham's car and man – "but has the gentleman any clothes? I haven't a trunk of his."

She gave a start of dismay. He had brought absolutely nothing.

"They are coming on by train," she said. She had had to lie for him before, and now she must lie again, and she hated lying; even little lies were abhorrent.

"Will you get me some sandwiches and some coffee? There is a vacuum flask in the basket." She looked dubiously at her husband. "Do you think I could wake him?" she asked.

"I'll try if you like, madam," said the chauffeur dryly, and shook the sleeping man.

To her surprise Pretoria Smith woke up almost immediately, blinked round at the chauffeur and Marjorie, and his hand strayed mechanically to his waistcoat pocket.

"Hullo!" he said. "What has happened?"

He looked at the girl for a long time, and then it seemed to dawn upon him.

"So we're married, are we? I seem to remember it," he said thoughtfully. "Where are we?"

"Will you have some coffee?" she asked. "I don't think you're — very well."

"Coffee? Capital!" He was quite energetic. "I am afraid you thought I was rather a brute this morning, but I couldn't use — " his hand strayed again to his pocket — "what I wanted to use, and I sort of went — funny."

He drank the coffee greedily and seemed almost to recover. Then he passed his hand over his rough cheeks and murmured an apology.

"I'll walk about for a little while," he said, "and try to get the use of my legs."

He strolled up the road and back, and when he returned he was almost normal.

"I don't know how to begin to ask you your forgiveness," he said. "But the fact is, last night — "

"Please don't tell me," she interrupted him. "I — I don't want to know."

He flushed, looked at her queerly, then laughed.

"All right," he said, almost stiffly. (She rather liked him when he smiled.) "We'll let that matter rest."

She gave him some sandwiches but he declined them.

"I can't eat," he said with a shudder. "Perhaps later. What time do we reach Brightsea? I suppose we're on the way there?"

"In a little over an hour, sir," said the chauffeur, and Smith looked at his watch and whistled.

"It has stopped," he said, holding it to his ear. "What is the time?"

"Two o'clock," said the chauffeur, and Pretoria Smith seemed satisfied.

The car went on again and now he was talkative, though absurdly conscious of his unshaven and disreputable condition.

"There ought to be some clothing waiting for me at the cottage," he said. "I took the liberty of wiring to a tailor in London telling him to direct my stuff there. Is that all right?"

"Of course it's all right," she replied. "You're entitled to send your clothes to my house now," she said with a pathetic attempt to be amusing.

He looked at her.

"Then we *are* married?"

"Very much married," she said, and could not avoid the bitterness in her voice.

He spent a quarter of an hour apparently absorbed in the passing country.

"I like this place," he said after a while. "I wish I were not going back to South Africa."

"Are you going back?" she asked a little dismally. "I mean – are we going back?"

"*I* am going back," he said gently, "after a reasonable time." He lingered on the last two words, as though he were not sure what was a reasonable time.

"Do you love South Africa?" she asked. The news he gave her was cheering.

"I love it, in a way," he said.

"When – when will you be coming back," she asked, "after you go this time?"

Again that little smile illuminated his face.

"Oh, it may be years," he said.

"Do you really mean that?"

"Of course I mean it. I tell you, I love the place, and I love old Solomon. I think he's quite wrong in believing that he has only a short time to live. He's as hale and as hearty as any man I know. By the way," he said, turning to her suddenly, "he does not intend letting you wait until he dies before you benefit through your marriage."

"What do you mean?" she asked, surprised.

"His lawyers in London are authorized to place two hundred thousand pounds to your credit on your wedding day," he said, "and I asked – somebody – " he hesitated – "to send that wire just as soon as the ceremony was over."

"Two hundred thousand pounds!" she gasped.

He nodded.

"You have an account at the local bank, haven't you? That is where the money will go."

The girl drew a long, quivering sigh of relief. Her mother could settle with Lady Tynewood. And now for the first time she told her mother's secret. She wondered afterwards why she had done this, and excused her betrayal of Mrs Stedman's weakness in the words she introduced the subject.

"You are my husband now, so you ought to know these things. My mother owes a lot of money. Poor mother has only taken to these wild and gambling ways recently," she said with a little smile, "and I'm awfully sorry for her, because she's had so little fun in life."

"Gambling?" said Pretoria Smith. "Whom does she gamble with? Not with Lady Tynewood?" he asked sharply.

The girl nodded.

"Oh, indeed?" This time Pretoria Smith's smile was crooked, and it was not pleasant to look at.

"You hate Lady Tynewood, don't you?" she asked. "You can tell me, because I hate her too."

"What harm has she done to you?" asked her husband. "She's done enough to me in all conscience. She ruined – "

He checked himself and then with a shrug went on:

"I must give you confidence for confidence – or half-confidence perhaps would be more correct – she ruined a very dear friend of mine."

She looked at him quickly.

"Was it her husband?" she asked, and he inclined his head.

"It was her husband," he repeated "Do you know the story of Sir James Tynewood?"

"It is rather a sad one, isn't it?" asked Marjorie.

"I don't know whether it's sad or whether it's mad," he said. "I know it very well, and one of these days I will tell you – that I promise you. And on that day, Lady Tynewood will be a very sorry woman."

There was such a menace in his tone that the girl looked at him with a new interest. But he did not refer again to the subject until they had reached the cottage.

THE NIGHT OF THE WEDDING

It was a little bungalow set on the slope of a hill, surrounded by a new fence, over which the rambler roses were bursting into pink bloom. They found tea waiting for them, served by the elderly cook-housekeeper, and the afternoon was not unpleasantly passed. The girl had plenty of time to think, for Pretoria Smith spoke very little and seemed absorbed in his thoughts. He spent the greater part of the time before dinner wandering aimlessly about the garden, which overlooked the sea. They dined together, and then he was very little more talkative than he had been in the afternoon.

Marjorie's courage was gradually oozing under the strain; and when the housekeeper came in to ask if she could spend the night with her son, who was on leave from the Navy in Brightsea, she gave a revelation of this panic.

"No, no, no!" she said. "You can't go, you can't go, Mrs Parr! You must stay here!"

Pretoria Smith, who had been silent, looked up in surprise.

"Why, of course she can go, Marjorie," he said. "If the boy is home on leave from the Navy, she will want to see him, and leaves are very scarce in these days."

"I can't be left alone." Marjorie was almost hysterical. "I can't make fires and things!"

"There is no need to make fires, except the kitchen fire," he said, amused, "and I'll make tea in the morning."

"You can't go, Mrs Parr," said the girl doggedly. "I want you – I'm not feeling particularly well and my husband has been ill."

The elderly female looked from one to the other with a long face, and when she went out into the kitchen, Pretoria Smith followed her. He was gone about five minutes, and after a while Mrs Parr came in with the coffee and left them.

They were talking about nothing in particular when Marjorie heard the back door slam.

"What is that?" she asked.

"It's Mrs Parr gone home to see her boy," said Pretoria Smith coolly. "It was absurd of you to be frightened, Marjorie. The poor woman is just aching to see her son."

The girl felt herself shaking.

"All right," she said, mastering her fear — "as you wish."

There was something she wanted to say and now she felt beyond fear.

"I heard you ask Mrs Parr this afternoon to put a bottle of whisky in your room," she said.

He nodded, keeping his grave eyes on her.

"Well, I — I wish you wouldn't." She was very earnest.

He frowned.

"I'm sorry you've asked that," he said, "but if you would prefer that I didn't, you can have it in your room."

"I would much rather," she said. "You think I'm a prig, don't you?" and he laughed.

She endured two hours of agony, trying to make some sort of conversation, trying to interest herself rather than him in anything but this great, absorbing fact which was now dominating every other thought. She was married, had been married twelve hours, and this man who sat opposite to her, in the ill-fitting clothing, was her husband. At ten o'clock she interrupted the conversation.

"I'm going to bed now," she said, and without a word turned and went up the stairs.

She closed the door behind her and felt for the key, but there was no key, and then she remembered that her mother, who had a horror of fire, never allowed a key to be in any door. She searched frantically in her bag for her key ring, but there was nothing upon that which would lock the door, and she sat down on the bed and stared hopelessly at the floor.

She was really tired. The events of the day had shaken her more than she had imagined. But she could not sleep. She lay on one side, listening all the time, and presently she heard his feet on the stairs, and caught her breath. They passed her door, and she heard the door of his room close gently, and breathed again.

She waited for half an hour, for an hour, but no sound came. A clock tower in distant Brightsea struck one, and still she waited, watchful, restless, sleepless and alert. And then nature overcame her and she dozed. It was a restless sleep, broken by unpleasant dreams, but at last she fell into a sound untroubled slumber and her tired frame relaxed.

She woke with a start, pushed her fair hair from her eyes and sat up in bed. She had heard a sound. What it was she could not fathom. But her heart was beating wildly. Then she heard it distinctly – the creak of a board in the passage outside. Somebody was moving. She could hear their heavy breathing, and, fascinated, watched the door. Presently she saw the handle turn slowly, for she had left her light burning. Slowly, slowly it turned, and then the door opened inch by inch, as though the intruder was fearful of awaking her. Pretoria Smith crept slowly into the room. He was wearing a dressing-gown and as he walked he swayed to and fro.

He looked stupidly at the bed, and his eyes travelled slowly up until they rested upon the white face of the girl.

"What do you want?" she breathed. The bed shook beneath her.

"I want that whisky," he said thickly, and she stared at him.

"No, no," she quavered, trying to humour him. "You mustn't have any more, you really mustn't. You've had so much and I thought you told me you would send the bottle to my room."

"I want that whisky," he repeated, like a child saying a lesson. "It is in your room – I put it there this evening."

Her eyes strayed to the wash-stand and to her amazement the bottle was there.

It's the only thing that will stop it," he mumbled.

He lurched and would have fallen, but caught the edge of the bed. She slipped out of bed on the opposite side and drew on her dressing-gown.

"I will bring it to you," she said. "Please go. I will bring it to your room."

"It's the only thing now," he said and drew himself up till he lay full length on the bed. "My God! My head, my head!"

She looked at him with a new wonder.

"Are you ill?" she asked, and he nodded.

"Mother keeps some medicine here."

She walked across the room in her bare feet, and her legs felt dreadfully weak. There was a little medicine cupboard above the washstand, and she opened it with shaking fingers.

"But you mustn't have any more drink. What would you like?"

"Have you any quinine?" he asked.

She took a little bottle of pellets from the cupboard and brought them across.

"Yes, here are some."

"Thank God!" he said, snatching at the bottle.

"But you mustn't drink," she repeated.

"Drink? My dear, good soul," he said wearily, "I haven't tasted a drink for eight years."

She could hardly believe her ears.

"But you were drunk on the night of the dinner."

"Drunk?" He chuckled feebly, dropped three pellets in his hand, and, throwing back his head, swallowed them at a gulp. "Get me some water, can you, please?"

She brought him a glass and he drank greedily.

"Haven't had a drink for eight years," he repeated. "Drunk at the Prince's dinner was I, Marjorie? Ask the Prince! Didn't you hear us talking in the Swahili language? We're old shooting friends, that is why he was so decent."

She gasped, remembering the gibberish he had talked as he lay across the Duke's table.

119

"I had malaria," he went on, "and have had it since I have been in this country. I'm rotten with it, I always am this month."

"Malaria?" she whispered, as the truth of the matter began to dawn on her. "And you've never – never been drunk? You weren't, not – when you married me?"

He smiled.

"That's fine," he said, and passed his hand over his forehead. "The headache has gone immediately. Drunk at your wedding?" He chuckled again. "I took almost a fatal dose of strychnine to brace myself up for that wedding," he said. "Feel my hand."

She took his hand in hers and uttered a cry. It was so hot that it seemed to burn her.

"I've a temperature of a hundred and five, it will amuse you to know," he said feebly. "If I had some hot coffee – "

She flew out of the room and down the stairs; and her busy fingers were lighting a fire before she realized that she had told the absent Mrs Parr that she hated lighting fires. She brought him back some coffee. He was still lying on the bed, and she drew the clothes over him.

"You'll rest there till the morning," she said authoritatively. "I suppose your fever isn't catching?"

He looked at her with that queer smile of his.

"No more catching than – drink," he said, and with this little jest he smiled himself into a long, deep sleep. And the girl sat by his side, watching him, as she had sat and seen yet another dawn come up out of the east. All her doubts were now set at rest and the last vestige of suspicion had been dissipated.

For in her heart of hearts she had believed that the killer of Sir James Tynewood whose body lay under another man's name in the chapel at Tynewood Chase, was Pretoria Smith.

LADY TYNEWOOD PURSUES HER ENQUIRIES

"My husband has now quite recovered from his attack of fever. He has been suffering from malaria ever since he arrived in this country, and I am afraid I am as responsible as anybody for the impression which seems to prevail, that the poor man drank. I have written to Lord Wadham and to the Duke, to tell them just what happened on the night of the dinner. We shall be coming home the day you receive this, so will you please have my room and the spare room ready. My husband wished to stay at the inn, but of course that is impossible…"

Here Mrs Stedman interrupted her reading with a succession of "H'ms" which meant that she had reached a portion of the letter which should not be read aloud.

Alma Tynewood, however, had seen her own name, for, although she sat by the side of the reader, she had excellent eyesight.

"And that is all, my dear," said Mrs Stedman artlessly as she folded the letter in some haste and put it into her writing-case.

"So the happy pair are coming home and he doesn't drink, or at least his devoted wife says he doesn't," said Alma Tynewood thoughtfully. "It is rather touching!"

"I do hope they will be happy," sighed Mrs Stedman, shaking her head mournfully as though she had no hope at all upon the subject.

"Happy!" Lady Tynewood was amused. "That kind of man could not make any girl happy," she said with unusual vehemence, "and I'm not so certain that Marjorie – " She checked herself. "However, we shall see. I am most anxious to be friendly with Marjorie if she will give me half a chance."

It was true that she was anxious to be friendly with Marjorie, for Marjorie was a very rich woman and was an inexhaustible reservoir, from whence Alma Tynewood and her friend could supplement their incomes, if Mrs Stedman continued upon her speculative career.

"Marjorie is a good girl," said the complacent Mrs Stedman, smoothing her dress. "Of course, there are times when she's very trying, but I think that is not unusual in the modern girl."

Lady Tynewood looked across her poised teacup.

"Marjorie used to go to work once, didn't she?" she asked carelessly and Mrs Stedman shivered.

"Yes," she answered, with some reluctance. "Of course, we weren't always as well off. Before dear Solomon repaid the money which he borrowed from my husband we were very poor indeed."

It was a fiction of hers that Solomon's generosity was in the nature of a repayment. Mrs Stedman's pride was of the type which refused to admit her obligations. Gratitude was incompatible with the maintenance of her self-respect – she was too proud to be thankful. Therefore had she invented a loan advanced by her impecunious husband to a man who had taken nothing and given everything, and she felt in consequence that comfortable feeling which mean-minded people experience as they contemplate their "independence."

"Yes, my dear, we had a terrible time," she said, for now she had disposed of the suggestion that her present affluence was due to anything but the tardy repentance of a debtor and she could afford to magnify her own hardships.

"Marjorie used to work for a firm of lawyers, Vance & Vance, a very respectable firm in the city. Mr Vance used to be my husband's solicitor, and Marjorie was quite a favourite of his. Of course, she never did the menial things that girls in offices usually do."

"Such as carrying messages?" suggested Lady Tynewood.

"Oh dear no," said the shocked Mrs Stedman. "Mr Vance was very sorry to lose her, but I was glad when she left. Two nights in succession, my dear, she came home late, so white and shaking that I thought I should have to call the doctor in. The last time she had been into the country on a very important and confidential errand and when she got back to our – er – little flat she collapsed. I remember it very well," said Mrs Stedman, turning her head, "because it was that night I received from my brother-in-law, dear Solomon Stedman, a draft for a large sum of money."

"He had found his mine, eh?" smiled Lady Tynewood.

"No, no, my dear, he didn't find the big mine for months afterwards," corrected Mrs Stedman, "but he had found the – what was the word? Leader, that's the word. He had found the leader which eventually brought him to his present wonderful discovery."

Mrs Stedman had the vaguest ideas on gold mining, but she knew enough to convey to Lady Tynewood just what had happened.

"Did your daughter ever tell you of what she had seen, or what her experience had been those two days?" asked Lady Tynewood carelessly. "I mean the days she came home so upset?"

Mrs Stedman shook her head.

"Marjorie never tells me things," she said. "She is a most reticent girl and, remembering that I am her own mother, I think it is a little hard that I should be kept in the dark. When I was a girl, I told my dear mother everything."

Lady Tynewood was thinking rapidly.

"Was Mr Vance the lawyer a great friend of Marjorie's?" she asked.

Mrs Stedman nodded.

"He was very good to Marjorie, though of course he couldn't very well be anything but good to the daughter of a lady who was the wife of an old client – "

"Did he ever communicate with her after she left the office?"

Mrs Stedman looked up in surprise.

"Why, Alma," she said with a little smile, "what a queer question to ask! Why are you so interested in our struggles?"

Lady Tynewood laughed.

"I am interested," she said. "I am curious to know what relationships continue between an employer and his – " she was at a loss to find a word which would not offend Mrs Stedman, who would have bitterly resented the use of the word "servant" – "and his – his former colleagues after their business relationships have ceased."

"Well, it is rather curious you should have asked that question," said Mrs Stedman slowly, "because I always had the impression that Mr Vance and Marjorie had some secret in common. Of course," she said with an assumption of motherly virtue, "there was no question of Mr Vance being in love with Marjorie, because he was fifty or more and he had a wife and six children, which wholly precluded such a possibility."

Drawing from a larger experience of life, Alma did not preclude that possibility in principle but was willing to concede the point in this particular case.

"I know that Marjorie was worried," Mrs Stedman went on, "and once when I let fall a perfectly innocent remark, she turned as pale as death."

"What was that innocent remark?" asked Lady Tynewood, trying to keep all traces of eagerness from her tone.

"Now, let me see," continued the older woman knitting her forehead. "Oh yes, I remember – I happened to say that Dr Fordham's housekeeper had taken a cottage at the other end of the village."

"Dr Fordham's housekeeper?" repeated Lady Tynewood slowly. "Who was Dr Fordham?"

"I don't know him at all," replied the other, shaking her head, "but he used to live about here some time ago. He died of influenza and his housekeeper came to Tynewood to settle down. I believe Sir James gave her a cottage. My dear, you must know something about that," she said archly.

"I don't know anything at all about it," replied Lady Tynewood, "but where is this cottage? Is she still living there?"

Mrs Stedman nodded.

"I asked Marjorie what there was about Dr Fordham which could possibly interest her, but in her secretive way – and, my dear, there's no other word to describe Marjorie's reticence – she changed the subject."

"What is the name of Dr Fordham's housekeeper?

"A Mrs Smith," replied the hostess a little impatiently. "Really, Alma, you are the most persistent person. How can this woman possibly interest you? Oh yes, of course," she added apologetically, "it is one of Sir James's cottages and naturally – "

Lady Tynewood rose and laid her cool hand on Mrs Stedman's. Though she was in no apparent haste her car moved all too slowly for her. She found Mr Augustus Javot wandering in the garden, a very bored man. Briefly she related her conversation with Mrs Stedman and what she had learnt.

"Better leave well alone," said Javot warningly. "Why stick your nose into affairs that don't concern you?"

"Are you mad?" she asked angrily. "Don't you realize what it means to you and to me if James is dead?"

He scratched his chin.

"I realize a good many things," he said significantly. "Some of 'em seem to have turned your clever little brain."

She had seated herself on a garden seat and was examining the gravel path abstractedly.

"If James is dead," she said slowly, "Tynewood belongs to me. And if he died as I think he died, then this swine, Pretoria Smith, has got to pay the price!"

"Leave well alone," murmured the peace-loving Augustus Javot. "You're on a good thing and you've only to sit tight and enjoy life."

"Life!" she scoffed. "Do you call this life? Buried away in a rotten little country village raising pigs and chickens! I'm sick of all this, Javot. I want to go back to London, and I want to go back with money for a town house and cars. I want to give parties like we used to give."

"There's no reason why you shouldn't go back to London and have a little flat – " began Javot.

"A little flat!" she cried wrathfully – "and be the laughing-stock of the old crowd! Molly Sinclair and Billie Vane! What do you think they will say if I come back to London and play the game small? Do you think I'm staying in this miserable village because I love the life? No, it is only because I cannot cut the shine which I am entitled to cut and have the money which is mine by right, that I stay here at all. I had a letter from Molly the other day asking me why I didn't invite her down to Tynewood. She thinks I'm at the Chase. So do they all. I'm not going back to London to be made look a fool."

Again Mr Javot scratched his chin.

"You could be made look a pretty bad fool in Tynewood," he said, and with an angry "Pshaw!" she turned and left him.

Mr Javot smiled to himself and lifted a dead leaf from a rose-bush.

"This is the life," he said, and honestly meant it.

THE RETURN FROM BRIGHTSEA

The journey from Brightsea had a charm and a quality which the journey to Brightsea had not possessed for the girl. And the well-tailored athletic figure that sat by her side was a different man to the fever-stricken Pretoria Smith who had slept uneasily in the corner of the limousine on her wedding day. And if Marjorie Smith was not a riotously happy woman she was at least a peaceful one, for she had faith in this husband of hers, and faith and confidence are the best, and the only adequate, substitutes for love. If she had not found a husband, she had at least gained a friend, and a friend in whom she reposed greater and greater confidence as the days progressed.

"I am so glad you have agreed to stay at the house," she said, apropos of nothing. She had broken a long silence, which had followed his description of the bush-veld.

"If you had gone to the inn, people would have — talked."

He nodded.

"Mother may be a little — trying," she said, loyalty to her mother and her desire to prepare him, struggling for mastery. "She is really very sweet and kind, but she is a little tactless at times."

"I think I know," he said.

"And then there is Lady Tynewood," she went on, wishing to get it all over at once. "She is rather a frequent visitor. I hope you won't mind."

He turned to her with a little smile.

"I am rather ashamed of my outburst, that morning," he said. "But in excuse I can bring forward my young friend, M A Laria, Esquire. He was very active and rampageous that morning, but I owe Lady

Tynewood an apology, at least I did until this morning," he corrected himself, "when I wrote to her."

"You wrote to her?" she said in surprise, and dropped her hand on his. "That's good of you," she said with a kindling of her eyes. "I don't like Lady Tynewood any more than you, but she is mother's friend, and a very poor friend, I'm afraid," she said with a wry smile. "Mother likes her."

"I shall be most polite to Lady Tynewood," said Pretoria Smith impressively. "I shall take my coat off and lay it in the puddles that her dainty feet shall not be wet, and I will meet her at the door on my knees and tap my head three times on the ground, and every night and morning I will burn a joss stick."

"You're being silly," she said, but felt happy.

They came to her mother's house and Mrs Stedman, assuming the benevolent but distant attitude which she felt that the character of mother-in-law called for, met them at the porch and gave them a polite welcome.

"I have your rooms ready," she said. "I could not think of giving Mr Smith the spare room which is at the other end of the house, my dear" – she patted her daughter's cheek – "so I gave him my room, which is next to yours."

"Oh, mother," said the girl in dismay, "you haven't turned out of your room – "

"No sacrifice is too great for my daughter," smiled Mrs Stedman, "and really I'm not at all uncomfortable, though of course I miss my own bed, or rather shall miss it," she corrected herself.

"You're going straight back, mother," said the girl determinedly. "I will not allow you to inconvenience yourself. My husband doesn't mind the spare room, even if it is at the other end of the house, do you – John?"

Pretoria Smith, secretly amused, shook his head.

"I should really prefer a room over the stable," he said gravely. "You must remember, Mrs Stedman, that I am not used to the luxuries of this gentle life. Or," he went on, in spite of the girl's appealing and anguished glance, "a shake-down in the summer house, or a camp bed in the conservatory amongst the earwigs, would be welcome. I miss the spiders in the morning and am lost when I fail to find a stray scorpion or two in my blankets."

Mrs Stedman listened open-mouthed. Pretoria Smith to her was a dour, silent man. This was the picture she had formed of him and she was most anxious not to change it. She hated change.

"I shall certainly not go back to my room," she said, the sacrificial spirit bright within her. "The spare room is a little damp and I could not think of allowing your husband to occupy a damp room."

"Mother—" began the girl.

"Of course," said Mrs Stedman thoughtfully, "your room is a very big one, my dear, and when I was a young married woman there was never a question of two rooms. One large room and a dressing-room, yes, but—"

Pretoria Smith came to the rescue.

"Mrs Stedman," he said sombrely, "you either move back to your own room and give me that damp spare room or I will go to an inn and scandalize the neighbourhood. Think what people would say if it is known that we are married, and are parted so soon."

This was an argument not to be dismissed lightly and Mrs Stedman demurred, but yielded.

"Phew!" said Marjorie, when he met her again in the drawing-room and they were alone, "you weren't very helpful."

"I wasn't helpful?" he said indignantly. "Well, I like that! But for me, the customs of the mid-Victorian age would have been revived – without the dressing-room!"

She looked at him queerly and laughed.

"You're a strange man," she said, "but we shan't be here long, shall we? You talked of going to London."

"I am going to London," he said quietly. "I have a lot of things to buy to take back with me."

"Take back with you?" she repeated. "You mean to South Africa? When are you sailing?"

"Next Saturday week," he replied, and there was a silence.

"You didn't tell me you were going back so quickly?"

"I kept that good news as a surprise for you," said Pretoria Smith, and again there was a long pause.

"Next Saturday week," she said, half to herself, and then: "How long will you be away? Don't read that paper, it's rude when I'm asking you questions."

He put down the paper with a little laugh.

"It may be for years and it may be for ever," he said lightly.

"Then I'm to be – " She did not finish the sentence.

"You're to be a nice good girl," said Pretoria Smith quietly, "until I can persuade old Solomon that this marriage was altogether ridiculous and unnecessary."

"And then?" she asked quietly.

"Then you can divorce me," he said. "I hate that you should do it, or have the bother of it, but an undefended case attracts very little publicity."

"And you'll give me cause?"

He nodded.

"It sounds rather horrible, doesn't it" she asked with a little shiver, "but I don't think I want a divorce. I mean I shall be perfectly content, for there is nobody I want to marry – but you may want to marry somebody," she added quickly.

"That is unlikely," said Pretoria Smith, "extremely unlikely."

She strolled to the window and opened it and remembered, oddly enough, that it was through this window she came uttering her determination that she would not marry Pretoria Smith, and stepped out into the garden.

She had a curious sense of loss and tried to analyse the feeling. Yes, it was because Pretoria Smith was going away and because she liked him. He had been so kind to her and so friendly, and she liked his humour and his clean view of things. She had never had a man friend, except Lance. Her lips curled, whether at the thought of Lance or at the comparison between the two men it was hard to judge, harder for her because she did not pursue her analysis so far.

Pretoria Smith had joined her and was walking by her side.

"Then, after Thursday," she said, "I shan't see you again until you come to say goodbye."

"Is that necessary?" asked Pretoria Smith lighting a cigarette.

Marjorie shrugged.

"If you don't wish to come, you need not," she said. "There is really no necessity at all, and you'll be very busy."

"I'll come down if you wish," said Pretoria Smith quietly, and to this she made no reply.

Something of the colour and harmony of life had gone out, she felt. Perhaps it was because he made her realize her false position or revived the unpleasant memory of Solomon Stedman's ultimatum, but whatever was the cause she felt distressed and unhappy.

"Before you go," she said, "I want to unburden my mind of a secret."

He looked round at her sharply.

"Is there anybody else?" he asked quickly.

"Is there anybody at all?" she corrected, and he flushed.

"I meant that, of course," he replied stiffly. "We have neither harboured the illusion that there is anything in our friendship or our marriage but the humouring of an old man's caprice."

"Sit down here," she commanded, and on the very seat where she had received Solomon Stedman's letter less than a fortnight ago, she told him something that she had never told to any man or woman before.

It was a long time before she could speak, and when she did she came to the essence of the matter in a sentence.

"It is about Sir James Tynewood," she said. "I know that he is dead. And I know that you were with him when he died."

THE STORY OF SIR JAMES TYNEWOOD

Pretoria Smith made no comment. He lit another cigarette from the glowing end of the old one, put it on the ground and carefully placed his foot upon it.

"So Sir James Tynewood is dead," he said slowly, "and it is true that I have known for some time."

She did not speak and he went on a little bitterly:

"Also I know the woman who killed him."

She was at a loss how to go on now and he half turned to her and his kindly eyes were fixed upon hers.

"I want to hear your story," he said. "You rather startled me."

She began haltingly, but as the narrative proceeded she grew more and more coherent, and the man who sat beside her, staring into the flower beds before them, interrupted very seldom.

"When we were poor, before Uncle Solomon helped us," she said, "I used to work in a lawyer's office. I was secretary to Mr George Vance of Vance & Vance. He knew my father and was very good to me. I did most of the confidential work for the firm and in that capacity I received you when you returned from South Africa. You do not recall my face?

To her surprise he nodded.

"Very well," he said, "please go on."

"The day you came back he sent for me, and to my surprise he handed me an envelope which evidently contained a letter that he had typed himself. It was addressed to Sir James Tynewood, Baronet, 947 Park Mansions.

" 'Miss Stedman,' he said, 'I want you to do me a great favour. I hate using you as a messenger, but in this particular case it is necessary that somebody should take this letter, somebody whom I can rely upon.'

"He explained to me that the address was a flat belonging to an actress named Alma Trebizond, who was a member of a very fast theatrical set.

" 'You will find Sir James there,' he said, 'and I want you personally to deliver this letter, and if possible, bring back an answer. I am also relying upon you to keep secret anything which may happen or anything which you may see or hear.'

"I was very much surprised. I had never undertaken such a mission before, but of course I was quite willing to go. It was at half-past five in the evening when this letter was given to me and it was quite dark when I arrived at the building, which is a very large block of flats overlooking Regent's Park. I was taken up in the lift to the floor and found the door without difficulty. Even before I rang I could hear that there was an awful commotion going on inside. A piano was playing and it was some time before I could make myself heard, and then a servant came and I went into the hall. There was evidently a party in progress for I could hear two or three people singing at once.

"Presently I was shown into the room and Sir James came forward.

" 'What do you want?' he asked.

"I told him that I came from Vance & Vance and that I had a letter which had to be delivered personally to him. He took the letter with a curse, opened it and read it, and then swore. He had been drinking and had taken too much.

" 'You can tell Vance he can go to hell,' he said, 'and you can tell Jot that he can go to hell too.'

"And then he laughed and before I knew what he was doing a man had clasped me round the waist and tried to make me dance.

"That was when I saw Alma Trebizond for the first time. I don't know how I escaped from that room. A man helped me get away – I think now it must have been Mr Javot," said the girl with a shudder. "They wanted me to dance, they wanted me to drink. The man who

133

held me kissed me and Sir James took no further notice of my presence. But I did get out eventually and went straight back to the office where Mr Vance was waiting for me and told him what had happened. I even delivered the message," she smiled.

"What did Vance say?" asked Pretoria Smith.

"He was very much upset," replied the girl, "and he again asked me not to mention a word of what I'd seen or heard. I thought that as Sir James was his client he was anxious that I should not think badly of the young man."

"And then I came," said Pretoria Smith. "What happened the next day?"

"That afternoon Mr Vance sent for me again and he had typed another letter," said the girl.

"'I hate asking you to carry these messages, Miss Stedman,' he said, 'but I want you to go down to Droitshire to Sir James Tynewood's house and see Dr Fordham, who is a friend of Sir James, and give him this letter.'

"I reached Dilmot station about eight o'clock in the evening and Mr Vance had arranged for a car to meet me. I drove up to Tynewood Chase, and when I told my business I was immediately admitted through the gates.

"The house was in darkness and seemed to be empty, but I drove up to the big front door and there was a glimmer of a light showing. I rang the bell several times before the door was opened by a gentleman whom I learnt at once was Dr Fordham.

"'What do you want?' he asked sharply, and seemed disinclined to admit me, even to the hall, but it was raining heavily and he couldn't very well keep me on the doorstep" – she smiled – "so with some reluctance he let me come in.

"'I have a letter for Dr Fordham,' I said.

"'I am Dr Fordham,' he replied, and taking the letter, opened it and read it.

"He uttered an exclamation before he was halfway through.

"'Just sit down here for a moment,' he said, pointing to a chair. 'I will not keep you very long.'

"He passed through a door, which opened from the hall, and closed it behind him. Then the door was opened and I heard voices, one of which I recognized as Sir James Tynewood's. He was talking angrily, wildly I thought, but there is no need to tell you what he was saying. The other voice was – yours!"

Pretoria Smith said nothing. He threw away his smoked cigarette and coolly and deliberately took out his case and chose another.

"Go on," he said.

"I wondered what was wrong and was still wondering when suddenly I heard a shot. I was terrified, but I was curious. I think I also wondered whether I could be of any assistance. I walked to the door, which was open, and looked in and there I saw – " Her voice shook.

"There you saw?" repeated Pretoria Smith.

"Sir James Tynewood was lying on the floor in a pool of blood," said the girl in a low voice. "I saw the glint of a revolver and I saw a man leaning over him and heard him speak."

There was a silence.

"What did he say?" asked Pretoria Smith in a voice that was scarcely above a whisper.

"He said: 'My God! I have killed him!' " said the girl slowly, "and then he turned his head and I saw his face – it was you!"

Pretoria Smith blew a ring of smoke in the air.

"Well," he said, "what happened then?"

She described her drive in the dark with the doctor, and his words.

"That was all," said the girl. "I went back to Mr Vance and I told him. It was very late when I reached London, but he was waiting for me on the platform, and when I had described the scene I had witnessed he said that Sir James was not dead. He begged me not to speak to a living soul about the tragedy and I have kept my word until now."

Pretoria Smith rose.

"So you think I killed Sir James, do you?"

She shook her head.

135

"No, I don't think so now," she said quietly. "Of course, when I saw in the papers that Sir James had gone abroad and that it was his younger brother who had died of typhoid, I knew that Dr Fordham had given a false certificate because Sir James did not have a brother."

"A half-brother," said Pretoria Smith. "How did you work it out to your satisfaction? I mean what solution to that mystery did you find?" he asked, looking at her.

She shook her head.

"Not a very satisfactory one, I'm afraid. Rather on the romantic side. I think Sir James shot himself, and that in order to save the family from that stigma his brother went abroad and Sir James was buried in his brother's name."

"Does it occur to you that if that were the case," said Pretoria Smith after a moment's thought, "that the brother would one of these days turn up again and claim the estate?"

"I didn't think he could – he was only a half-brother," she replied quietly. "I thought the idea was that he'd pass quietly out of recognition and knowledge and that the family estate would go to – " she paused.

"To the Lady Tynewood?" he said quietly. "That is hardly likely. But who is that half-brother?"

She looked up at him quickly.

"If there is a half-brother, it is you," she said, and he nodded.

"You have shown powers of deduction worthy of the greatest detective," he mocked.

THE PHOTOGRAPH

Lady Tynewood had one of those restless and indefatigable natures which invite opposition in order to overcome the obstacles they call into being.

Mr Javot might be content with an acre of roses and two acres of kitchen garden, but Alma Tynewood's predilections lay in another direction. On the day that Mr and Mrs Pretoria Smith returned, she drove her car through the village to call upon another Mrs Smith. The housekeeper to the late Dr Fordham lived in a pretty cottage set back from the road and was sunning herself in placid contentment when Lady Tynewood knocked at her door.

The woman came through the cottage and curtsied to the visitor, whom she recognized, and Alma, watching her very closely for some sign of antagonism, decided that Dr Fordham had not taken his servant into his confidence to the extent of setting her against the wife of his friend.

Alma followed the obsequious Mrs Smith to the sunny garden in the rear of the cottage and accepted the Windsor chair which her flustered hostess carried out.

"I don't often have visitors, my lady," she said.

"I didn't know you were living here, Mrs Smith," smiled Alma, "otherwise I should certainly have called upon the housekeeper of my old friend, Dr Fordham."

Alma could lie very graciously and easily, and Mrs Smith accepted this claim to friendship with her dead master all the more willingly since she knew very little about the man she had served for ten years.

Gently and with great subtlety Lady Tynewood led the conversation towards Dr Fordham, and Mrs Smith was ready to talk.

"He was a strange man," she said. "I don't suppose I had a dozen words with him all the time I was in his service. He used to go abroad a great deal," she explained.

"Had he any relatives?" asked Alma.

The woman shook her head.

"No, ma'am," she said, "not a one."

"But who inherited his property when he died?"

"He hadn't much, my lady," said Mrs Smith, "and he left all that to me on his death-bed. About £300 and a few odds and ends of furniture. He didn't own the house we lived in. That belonged to Sir James, but Sir James kindly presented me with this cottage, at least his lawyers did."

"He must have been a very interesting man," said Alma. "Did he write books?"

Mrs Smith, who in spite of her employer's generosity had never regarded him as being particularly interesting, shook her head.

"No, my lady, he left very few papers, and those I've got upstairs. They're little accounts of travels he's made, a diary or two and a few other papers like his medical diplomas."

Alma Tynewood was disappointed. She had hoped that Fordham's housekeeper would have known more about him and would have had something to tell which would throw a light upon the mystery of Sir James Tynewood's disappearance. Failing that, she had no expectation of discovering documentary evidence, for a man in Dr Fordham's position would hardly be likely to leave papers or other written evidence of the part he had played.

"I've often thought," Mrs Smith went on, "that I should have sent the business papers to the lawyer, and again and again I've been going to do them up in a parcel and post them to Mr Vance – I only came across them after I'd turned out an old box of his."

Alma hesitated, and was on the point of going.

"I suppose that the diary deals with his trips abroad," she said.

"Yes, my lady. Would you like to see them? I'll show them to you. I know you will be interested."

She bustled off and came back with a faded plush-covered box and, laying it on her knees, opened it.

"Here's one, my lady." She handed the visitor a small but bulky pocket-book and Alma glanced through it.

It was full of strange names and unfamiliar places. One entry she saw which interested her.

"Whilst Jot and I were following the trail of a lion we came upon the track of another sportsman. This proved to be no less than the Duke of Wight, who we had heard was hunting in this country. The duke is a jolly good sort and Jot and he got on famously."

Who was Jot? The nickname of some acquaintance, she gathered. She glanced haphazard through the little volume, skipping the entries but finding nothing that informed her in the matter she was investigating.

"These are his two medical diplomas, my lady," said Mrs Smith; "they're all in Latin."

Lady Tynewood shook her head.

"Is there nothing else?"

"Only a portrait, my lady. It is interesting because the doctor wrote on the back of it: 'The only portrait in existence,' but I don't know who it is."

Alma Tynewood took the photograph and read the inscription written in the crabbed writing. Then she turned it and started to her feet as she looked upon the pictured face.

"At last!" she said.

It was the portrait of her husband, Sir James Tynewood!

A MIDNIGHT VISITOR

Mrs Stedman had said that she was taking a long drive through the country, and Marjorie was surprised when her mother came back in no very amiable frame of mind as she and Pretoria Smith were taking tea on the lawn.

"Why, mother, I thought you were going to be very late," said the girl, as Pretoria Smith rose to carry a chair to the table.

"I didn't expect to come back so early," said Mrs Stedman petulantly, "and I do wish, Marjorie, you would get out of the habit of timing me in as though I were some factory worker. I hate the feeling that I am being spied upon."

"That's rather strong, mother," smiled the girl. "What has happened? You seem cross."

"I am not cross, my dear. I am in a perfectly equable frame of mind," said Mrs Stedman tartly. "If I am a little put out I hope I am enough of a lady to hide my feelings. Really Alma is very inconsiderate."

"Did you go to the Tynewoods?" asked the girl quietly.

"Yes, I did go to the Tynewoods," said the defiant Mrs Stedman. "I shall go just where I like, Marjorie, and I will not have my own daughter correcting me, and certainly not before strangers."

"Hardly a stranger, Mrs Stedman," said Pretoria Smith cheerily, "I am one of the family now, you know."

"I beg your pardon, Mr Smith." Mrs Stedman was extremely polite. "I should not have said 'stranger,' for you are certainly more considerate to me than is Marjorie at times. I went to the Tynewoods to see Alma on a purely private matter which had nothing whatever to do with certain things which Marjorie doesn't like. And Alma was all excited and agitated as I've never seen her before. She told me she wasn't going to play this afternoon."

Mrs Stedman forgot for the moment the business-like character of her visit.

"Naturally I asked her why, and she told me that she'd made a great discovery and that she and Mr Javot were going to be extremely busy. In fact, my dear," said Mrs Stedman, raising her eyebrows and shaking her head, "Alma was positively rude."

Marjorie said nothing. She could only hope that Alma Tynewood had been rude to a point beyond forgiveness.

"And what was her great discovery?" bantered Pretoria Smith. "Has she found a new way of effacing wrinkles? It couldn't have been a new way of dealing aces from the bottom of the pack," he said, "because Javot taught her that years ago."

Mrs Stedman looked at him in astonishment.

"Dealing aces from the bottom of the pack?" she said incredulously. "Why, that would be cheating!"

"It would rather," said Smith easily, "and it would be clumsy cheating which could readily be detected, by anybody but a – a novice," he said.

"I'll never believe that of Alma," Mrs Stedman shook her head. "Never, never! You're prejudiced against Lady Tynewood, Mr Smith, and I deeply regret that your prejudice is shared by Marjorie, for no earthly reason. Unless of course," she said with a little self-pitying smile, "it is because Alma has shown a very marked preference for my society."

"You can believe it or believe it not," said Pretoria Smith, "but if you wish I'll show you how it is done. Bring me a pack of cards and I will undertake to deal myself all the aces and kings in the pack – and you shall shuffle!"

Mrs Stedman was annoyed, because she was ready to be annoyed with anybody or anything.

"You may be able to do that, Mr Smith," she said with acerbity, "but I do not think that dear Alma has had your training."

141

"Mother!" reproved the girl, but Pretoria Smith was laughing softly and his humorous eyes were fixed upon his mother-in-law.

"She hasn't," he said; "but then, of course, she hasn't been frequenting the worst saloons in South Africa as I have been, gaining my living by my wits and the sharpness and dexterity of my beautiful hands," he said complacently looking upon hands which were particularly white and small. "She has done no more than –" He stopped himself and the hard look which had come to his face faded out.

"Why do you tease mother?" asked the girl after Mrs Stedman had gone to her room.

"Do I tease her? I'm sorry," said Pretoria Smith humbly enough, though he was laughing. "But Alma Trebizond is a crook, you know."

"I can't understand why you say that," said the girl, with a worried look. "I don't like Alma, but she's not that kind of woman, I should imagine."

"You don't imagine anything of the kind," said Pretoria Smith. "You know she cheats!"

The girl was silent, because she had said as much to Alma Tynewood's face.

Mrs Stedman came back a little more amiable, but her mind still full of Alma.

"I think she is making a great fuss about nothing, although I suppose it must have been a shock to her after all these years."

"A shock?" said Pretoria Smith quickly. "What do you mean, Mrs Stedman?"

"Finding the portrait of her husband," said the other. "Mrs Smith gave it to her. You know Mrs Smith was Dr Fordham's housekeeper and apparently she had the portrait by her and gave it to Alma. It's the only portrait dear Alma has ever seen –"

The girl was staring at her husband, but Pretoria Smith was on his feet and his face was deathly white.

"What is she going to do with the portrait?" he asked huskily.

"She is going to put it in the newspapers," said the complacent Mrs Stedman, conscious of the sensation she had created. "In an advertisement asking for information of Sir James's present whereabouts."

"Oh, she is, is she?" said Pretoria Smith softly, and without a word of apology left the group and walked rapidly to the house, leaving his wife and mother-in-law staring after him, open-mouthed.

It had indeed been a busy day for Lady Tynewood. Mr Javot, though nominally her secretary, was unequal to the fatigue and labour of literary composition and it had been left to Alma to prepare the advertisements which were to appear in the London and South African newspapers.

At ten o'clock that night Mr Javot rose and yawned.

"I'll leave you to it, Alma," he said, "I'm going to bed."

She nodded without looking round and again dipped her pen in the ink.

"I'll take that picture with me to my room," said Javot. "I shall be up before you in the morning and my mind will be rather fresher than it is at present."

She hesitated.

"All right," she said, and handed the picture over her shoulder.

Mr Javot looked at it and chuckled.

"The portrait of a mug," he said pleasantly, "though I oughtn't to speak ill of the dead."

"Do you think he's dead?" Alma turned in her chair.

"Sure!" said the other calmly. "He's not the kind of fellow who suffers in silence, who can go away and stay away. He's the kind of weakling that would come back after a few months and cry on your shoulder! Besides, he's the head of a family. Suppose he did take his brother's advice or was influenced by his brother, how long would that last?

She was nibbling the pen-holder.

"There's a lot in what you say, Javot. You have streaks of intelligence."

"Thank you," he said sarcastically. "I'll put this picture under my pillow and sleep on it."

It was half-past eleven before Lady Tynewood gathered her papers into order, closed the desk and went up to her room. She shared Javot's suspicions, but those suspicions had to be proved facts before she could inherit Tynewood and all that Tynewood Chase meant.

She opened her solid-looking jewel case which stood on her dressing-table and then remembered that she had given the portrait to Javot, and relocked it. Half an hour later she was sleeping as soundly as the most virtuous.

At three o'clock she woke suddenly, which was unusual in her, turned over on the other side and was dozing again when she heard the sound again, the sound that had wakened her although she had not realized the fact. She sat up in bed, reached out her hand and switched on the light.

The man who was standing by her dressing-table turned quickly and there was a gleaming pistol in his hand.

"Don't shout," he said, "and don't scream."

She looked past him to the dressing-table. Her jewel-box was open, she could see the scarlet lining of the lid and a little electric handlamp was still alight in the man's other hand.

"What do you want?" she whispered huskily. "I have no money in the house and my jewels are at the bank."

She could not see his face. The lower portion was hidden behind a red silk handkerchief and the man still wore his felt hat and a long trench-coat which was turned up to his chin.

There was a patter of feet in the corridor without, the door opened and Javot blinked in.

At first he did not see the intruder.

"Are you talking in your sleep?" he began, and then his eyes fell upon the masked man.

"Put up your hands," said the burglar, and Javot obeyed. "Stand over there where I can see you."

The man carried the jewel-box to the bed and turned it out, sorting over the papers.

"Turn your faces the other way, both of you," he commanded, "I don't want you to see what I'm doing."

She heard the clink, clink, of trinkets, the rustle of papers, and once he uttered an exclamation. Then they heard the creak of a door and looked round.

The intruder was gone.

"Follow him," said the woman, "follow him!"

"Follow him yourself," said Javot coolly. "I am not in the habit of following burglars who carry a .38 Smith Wesson. Let him go and then we'll telephone for the police."

"You're a coward," she said.

"I'm a live coward," he said. "I'd rather be a live coward than a dead hero any day – or night," he added.

She was replacing the contents of her jewel case that had been spilt upon the bed.

"He has taken nothing," she said. "My rings are here – "

A door closed softly below.

"Now," said Mr Javot, "I'll do a little following," and presently she heard him speaking on the telephone.

A CUP OF TEA

That night Marjorie slept very badly. Possibly it was the thought of – no, it could not be that. The fact that Pretoria Smith was going back to South Africa ought not to worry her, and yet she could not help thinking of the curious position she would occupy after he had gone.

She would be another Lady Tynewood, she thought, a wife without a husband. A week ago that thought would have filled her with happiness and content. Today she saw only the disadvantages of the position and it worried her a little.

She put on the light and tried to read. Tynewood had an electric light plant of its own, the gift of a former baronet, and she had fixed a tiny electric kettle in her bedroom which on cold hunting mornings had proved a great blessing.

She got out of bed, put on her slippers and dressing-gown and filled the kettle from her water-bottle. She would make a cup of tea, she thought, and read for a while.

She settled herself in her armchair and tried to concentrate her mind upon *The Gentleman of France*. But every minute she found herself straying back to her own domestic problem. Was she to live here with her mother always, a wife in name, with a husband who did not wish to see her, and would probably write her polite letters at long intervals, inquiring after the state of her health!

Here again the prospect was not as alluring as it had been a week before, or a fortnight, she corrected herself. She had had a wild idea of suggesting to him that she should go to South Africa with him. She told herself that the voyage would benefit her, and then again she wanted to see strange lands. She could stay in Cape Town, or perhaps in Kimberley, and they need see very little of one another. And then, of course, she was most anxious to meet the relative who had forced this marriage upon her, old Solomon Stedman.

Marjorie Stedman and Marjorie Smith argued the matter out in her mind.

"My dear," said Marjorie Stedman, "you never wanted to see Uncle Solomon before, and when it was suggested to you two years ago that you should go to the Cape you said you hated the idea of a long sea voyage."

"That is true," admitted Marjorie Smith, "but I did not wish to travel alone, and Uncle Solomon had not made himself so important a factor in my life then."

On the whole the arguments of Marjorie Smith were extremely sound, but they did not convince Marjorie Stedman. She made her tea and poured herself a cup. She thought she heard somebody in the passage and went to the door in time to see Pretoria Smith disappear into his room.

She looked along at the closed door – it was at the far end of the corridor – in blank amazement. Perhaps he could not sleep either. She took another cup from the little cupboard and poured out a second cup of tea, and carried it along the corridor to his room and knocked.

"Who's there?" said the voice of Pretoria Smith.

"Marjorie," she answered.

She thought she heard him say: "Damn!" but hoped she was mistaken.

"Thank you very much," he said, opening the door. "Whatever are you doing at this hour of the morning?"

"What a question to come from you!" she laughed. "Have you been walking?"

"Yes, I have been for a little walk," he said.

His trench coat lay on the bed and her quick eyes noted a long blue sheet of paper on his dressing-table.

"I hope you'll sleep," she said awkwardly.

"I don't think I shall. Should we disturb your mother if I came and talked to you?"

"No," she said, her heart giving a little flutter. "I don't think so. Mother sleeps very soundly," and he followed the slim figure down the corridor, carrying his cup in his hand, and wondered why she went so quickly until he reached the room in time to see her straightening her bed.

"I'm awfully sorry," he said. "I really forgot that this was a bedroom."

Nevertheless he closed the door behind him and sat down, to rise again with a little grimace.

He put his hand in his hip-pocket and brought out to the girl's wondering eyes a small revolver which he laid on the carpet by the side of the chair.

"You needn't worry," he said. "It's not loaded. I never carry loaded revolvers in this country. There are so many people I want to kill that it would be a fatal temptation."

"But why ever do you carry it?" she asked. "Have you been committing a burglary?"

Her lips twitched as she asked the question and to her astonishment he nodded.

"I've been doing a little amateur burgling," he said calmly. "In fact, this is the second lady's bedroom I've been in tonight."

"You're not serious?" she said wide-eyed.

"I've made a call on Lady Tynewood. Open confession is good for the soul and a wife can't give evidence against her husband."

"But really?"

"I never tell a lie at three o'clock in the morning. It is the most truthful hour of the twenty-four for me," he said, stirring his tea. "One of these days I will tell you why I went there, but it was a visit not without profit."

She looked at the revolver dubiously.

"That isn't – "

"No, it isn't," he replied quickly, almost roughly. "My dear, of course it isn't!"

Only for a second had she wondered whether that was the weapon which had ended Sir James Tynewood's life.

"I've been thinking things over tonight," he said. "As a matter of fact, on my way back I did my biggest think. And it came to me in a rush that I have done you a very bad service, Marjorie."

"How?" she asked.

"By marrying you," said Pretoria Smith quietly. "Even to oblige old Solomon I should not have done it. It is rather terrible for you."

"And for you?" she asked.

He shrugged his broad shoulders.

"What difference does it make to me, except that I have on my conscience the unpleasant knowledge that I have probably wrecked your life."

"Then get it off your conscience," she said with a briskness and brightness which she was far from feeling. "It has tangled things a little, but then I don't see that it has made much difference to me. In all probability I should have lived on here until I was quite an old maiden lady, and I should have kept cats and parrots and an ancient coachman, and every Christmas I should have distributed blankets and coals to the poor."

"I don't think so," he said. "I mean," he added hastily, "I know you would have distributed blankets and coals, but I don't think you would have remained a maiden lady. But I don't want you to think too seriously of your unhappy position, Marjorie, because, because – because it may not come to a divorce."

"What do you mean?" she asked, her eyes fixed on his.

"I am going up country, when I return and settle things with Solomon. Into the Masai country, and probably I shall trek across Barotseland to the Belgian Congo – I want to have a shot at the Okapi. I'm not going willingly and knowingly and hopefully to commit suicide," he said with a faint smile, "but it is a queer country filled with all manner of pitfalls and dangers, even to the experienced traveller, and a man I met on the boat told me that twenty-five per cent of the people who go into that land do not come out again."

"Then you're not going," she said.

"Wait a moment," he was smiling. "It sounds rather as though I'm trying to harrow your feelings and work up a little cheap sympathy for my lonely lot. But that isn't the truth," he said seriously. "It is ninety chances in a hundred that I shall be one of the seventy-five who will get through with no more hurt than a sunburnt nose. I know you well enough to believe that you would not wish my death, even to secure your freedom, but there is that chance, and men like myself do not make old bones."

She nodded.

"And there is a chance too for you," she said.

"What do you mean?" he asked quickly.

"You know I have a weak heart and that one of my lungs is not all it should be."

He spilt the tea as he rose.

"You don't mean that?" he asked in agitation. "My dear girl, you shall go straight tomorrow to London and see a specialist. I know a tip-top man who would give you an opinion, and you ought to live in high country. Why not go to Switzerland, to Davos or Caux?"

And now he stopped because she was laughing at him, laughing till the tears showed in her eyes.

"You silly person," she said, "sit down. I'm the healthiest being in this country! But how do you like your feelings being harrowed? Of course, I know you would not wish for my death," she said gravely, "and it's ninety-nine chances in a hundred – "

He leant over and caught her by the ear, very firmly but very gently.

"You little devil!" he said, and that was all he said before he rose, picked up his gun and went back to his own room, but it left her tingling.

THE DENOUNCEMENT

"You know Lady Tynewood," said Mrs Stedman blandly.

This time Pretoria Smith took the outstretched hand.

"I know Lady Tynewood. I am afraid I was very rude to her the last time we met, and I hope that she's forgiven me," he said.

Alma smiled her sweetest.

"You had fever very badly I'm told, Mr Smith," she said.

"I had it very badly," said the other with a smile, and Mrs Stedman, bursting to tell the news, interrupted Alma's conventional expression of regret.

"Do you know that Lady Tynewood had a burglar in her house last night?"

"A burglar?" said Pretoria Smith. "That sounds thrilling! Did you kill him?"

"He got away unfortunately," said Lady Tynewood. "Mr Javot, my secretary, went after him."

"And shot him in his tracks?" said Pretoria Smith. "That's fine."

"No, he didn't shoot him." Alma was a little annoyed. "We missed him in the dark."

"Did you lose anything?" asked Pretoria Smith.

"Nothing at all," said Alma. "We disturbed him at his work. I have informed the police."

"What sort of man was he?"

"A rough-looking man," said Alma with a shrug. "I didn't see his face, which was masked, or rather covered with a handkerchief, but I think I should know his voice anywhere."

Her eyes were fixed on Pretoria Smith.

151

"Anywhere!" she repeated.

"Or anyhow," said Pretoria Smith. "That is fine. What do you think he was after, your jewels?"

Lady Tynewood did not know what the burglar was after. She only half suspected that the visitor had been Pretoria Smith and had debated this possibility with the sceptical Javot all the morning.

"It may be a man," she said slowly, "against whom I am collecting evidence and who thought that that evidence was in my possession."

"In that case," said Pretoria Smith lightly, "he should have broken into the police station or into Scotland Yard, or into the Church of St Giles, Camberwell," he added with a faraway look, and the colour left Lady Tynewood's face.

For a second she had no reply, then she turned to Mrs Stedman.

"Well, dear, I am going to the post office," she said. "I want to register this."

She held a thin parcel in her hand and it was securely bound with red tape.

"My dear, is that the portrait?" asked Mrs Stedman, all agog.

"That's the portrait," said Alma grimly. "And it is going to bring me to the position which I am entitled to occupy."

"That sounds romantic," said Smith. "Is it a friend of yours, Lady Tynewood?"

"My husband," said the woman, and Pretoria Smith raised his eyebrows and imparted into the movement just that shade of incredulity which was needed to bring the woman's irritation to a head.

Viciously she broke the tape and seals which bound the package and stripped off the brown paper.

"Do you know that man?" she asked, challenging him, and Pretoria Smith looked at the portrait for a very long time.

Then, before Alma Tynewood realized what had happened, he had taken it from her hand and under her eyes was tearing it into small pieces. With a hoarse cry of rage she leapt forward, but his strong arm pushed her back, gently but firmly, and then he turned and flung the fragments into the fireplace.

"I know that man," he said calmly, "but it is not your husband, Lady Tynewood."

The girl had watched the scene aghast. The audacity of the action, the flaming fury in Alma Tynewood's face, the cold smile on her husband's lips, the look of blank dismay in her mother, she took them all in in a flash, and they made a picture which was to be added to other unforgettable memories. And then Lady Tynewood fell back a pace.

"You shall pay for that, Mr Pretoria Smith," she said harshly.

"I shall pay a million times more than you will ever pay, though you deserve a million times more punishment," he said gravely, and then came a dramatic interruption.

The door opened quickly and a young man came in.

Marjorie had not seen Lance Kelman since her marriage and she stared at him now, for it seemed in that short time that his face had coarsened.

"Alma," he said, "I heard you were here and – " He stopped, feeling the tenseness of the scene. "What's the matter?" he said. "You got the portrait, didn't you?"

She did not reply, and then Lance saw Pretoria Smith.

"And I've got you," he said exultantly, and pointed an accusing finger at the man. "You're Norman Garrick, the half-brother of Sir James Tynewood, whom you murdered four years ago!"

TO SILENCE PRETORIA SMITH

It was Pretoria Smith who broke the silence which followed.

"Having said your little piece and created the requisite amount of sensation you can now make an exit before you're kicked out," he said, "and you can go with him, my friend," he addressed Lady Tynewood.

She was shaking in every limb, then she muttered: "He's dead. It's true!"

She turned and gripped Lance Kelman's arm.

"Come," she said, and they went out together.

Pretoria Smith walked to the window and watched them disappear down the drive, then turned with a laugh.

"Well, mother-in-law," he asked, "what do you think of that?"

Mrs Stedman did not know what to think. "It's very dreadful," she said, and felt it was a safe thing to say.

"Terrible!" said Pretoria Smith, and Mrs Stedman was on her dignity.

"We've never had anything like that in our family," she said.

"That's unfortunate," said Pretoria Smith. "We've had much worse things than that in our family! Two of my ancestors were hanged and one of them had his head cut off. So you may say that it runs in the family."

"Dreadful, dreadful!" Mrs Stedman shook her head helplessly. "It will be in all the newspapers."

"I don't mind the newspapers," said Pretoria Smith, "so long as it's not in the monthly magazines. But, seriously, Mrs Stedman, you ought not to worry, because there's nothing to worry about."

"I'm such a close friend of Lady Tynewood's," said Mrs Stedman dismally. "And it is extremely painful to me – "

"And you shall be a close friend of Lady Tynewood's all your life," said Pretoria Smith cheerfully. "Now please don't worry."

But Mrs Stedman was not prepared to forgo her gloom and went up to her bedroom to collect her thoughts, as she told them.

"Poor lady," smiled Pretoria Smith. "They will take a lot of collecting!"

"What does it mean? Are you Norman Garrick really?"

"No, I'm not Norman Garrick," he said quietly, "and there are times," he added with a whimsical smile, "when I don't know what I am or where I am." He drew a long breath. "I think I'd better get back to South Africa quick!" he said.

Curiously enough, the possibility of his leaving for South Africa was at that moment being discussed by a committee of three, of whom Mr Augustus Javot was the weary third.

"You want to get the warrant before he bolts," said Lance. "I know that type of bird! We've given him warning and the first thing we shall hear is that he's skipped."

"Wait a minute," said Javot. "Let's get this thing right. You say he's Norman Garrick, the half-brother of Sir James. How did you find that out?"

"It was a bit difficult," said Lance Kelman with a languishing glance at Lady Tynewood who was in no mood at that moment for tender glances. "It was inspiration, the inspiration I received from this dear lady which spurred me on, so to speak. It was the knowledge that I was helping her and putting her right in the eyes of the world that made me labour night and day – "

"Cut out all that stuff," said Javot calmly, "and tell us what you found."

The ruffled Mr Kelman swallowed something.

"Well, I'll tell you," he said. "I've been tracing the movements of Dr Fordham. He arrived in England the week you were married to Sir James." He addressed the girl. "I couldn't get the passenger list, but he came with a man who sailed a couple of days later by the outward steamer. The night before he sailed this other man stopped at the Grand Western Hotel, Southampton, because the sailing of the boat had been postponed. He was alone and registered his name as 'Norman Garrick.' It's written in the visitor's book."

"That was two days after I was married?"

"Well, I won't swear to the day," said Lance, "but it was as near as makes no difference, and after all a day or two doesn't matter. Anyway, he was registered at the hotel as Mr Norman Garrick and hired a car which took him to Tynewood Chase the same night. I've been able to trace that much from the local garage. Well, that was the extent of my discovery until I came back today and it occurred to me that I would call and see Mrs Smith, the housekeeper of Dr Fordham. You remember I came here first, Javot, and you told me that Lady Tynewood had seen this woman."

Javot nodded.

"Now, I went about my investigations in quite a different way to you, Alma," he said with a hint of patronage in his tone. "I didn't ask for documents, I came straight to the point and asked her if she remembered anything that happened four years ago and she told me – " he paused impressively – "that a gentleman had been shot at the Chase!"

"How did she know?" asked Alma quickly.

"She remembered that the doctor drove over in a taxi-cab to the house which was close to Tynewood Chase and got a lot of bandages and cotton wool and was in a very agitated state of mind. He told her that a gentleman had been shot, and after he returned and she asked him about the accident he said it was a slip of his tongue and he meant to say that the gentleman had died unexpectedly, the brother of Sir James. She didn't even know that Sir James's brother was ill. There were no servants in the house at Tynewood Chase, except the old lodge-keeper, because it was not occupied and Sir James seldom went down there."

"That sounds all right," said Javot thoughtfully. "But what is this rot about a warrant being out for Garrick, or whatever his name is?"

"Well," said Kelman a little discomforted, "I suppose the warrant will be out for him tomorrow when you make a statement to the police, Alma."

"Warrant nothing," said Javot, anticipating Lady Tynewood's reply. "There is going to be no warrant in this business, believe me. Now, what did he say about St Giles' Church, Camberwell?"

Lady Tynewood repeated the words that Pretoria Smith had uttered and Javot nodded.

"Go up and have a look at that jewel case of yours," he said significantly; "maybe you'll find something is missing."

She went up and returned in about a quarter of an hour with a drawn face.

"It's gone, has it!" said Javot grimly. "Well, my lady, I think you are in almost as bad a position as Pretoria Smith; in fact, if I had to make a bet about it, I'd back him to get away with all his trouble because the truth is beginning to dawn upon me."

He looked round at Lance Kelman, a puzzled young man, and added: "Perhaps you'll come in again this evening, Mr Kelman. I want to discuss a few private matters with Lady Tynewood."

"Of course, if I'm in the way," said Lance curtly as he rose, "I'll make myself scarce."

"You are a little in the way," said the other calmly. "Don't forget we dine at half-past seven."

Lance waited for Lady Tynewood to give him some encouragement to stay, but no encouragement came and he stalked forth, feeling ill-used and pardonably so.

"Now, Alma," said Javot, when he had gone, "I think we can come down to bedrock truth and face whatever is coming without illusions."

"What do you mean?" she asked, though she knew well enough all that his words implied.

"It means that Pretoria Smith has got your marriage certificate," said Javot, "and unfortunately it is not your marriage certificate to Sir James Tynewood, because that could be duplicated at the cost of a few shillings. It is the marriage certificate of a wedding which took place in St Giles', Camberwell, between one Augustus Javot, and one Alma Trebizond Johnson — and where you got Trebizond from, the lord knows, unless your father was an Armenian!"

She licked her dry lips.

"He wouldn't dare charge me with bigamy," she said. "We've got a pull on him now."

Javot shook his head.

"My dear wife," he said, "believe me, that kind of guy is difficult to get a pull on. He's simply made without hooks, and the best thing you can do is to go up to him in the morning and have a heart-to-heart talk with him."

"Talk to him!" she flamed. "Do you think I'm mad?"

"I shall think you're mad if you don't," he said. "Personally speaking, I love this little place, and I shall hate leaving it," he said, "but there is the fact, he has got us in his hand — or rather you, because I have committed no offence, unless it is an offence to condone your bigamy."

"I'll not do it," she said again, but she was quieter and calmer than he had expected.

"You must let me think this over, Javot. It means a lot more to me than to you."

She thought well into the night, and in the morning, to his surprise, she came early to breakfast wearing a tweed suit.

"You're up early."

"I'm going out to shoot rabbits," she said.

"What have the rabbits been doing to you?" asked Javot as he sliced off the top of an egg.

"I want some distraction," she said, "and I'm in a killing mood."

"Good luck to you," said Mr Javot pleasantly.

She avoided the main road and took the path across the fields which brought her to a lane, running at right angles from the road and incidentally forming the boundary line of Mrs Stedman's house.

Pretoria Smith saw her from the shade of a big yew tree, where he sat smoking his after-breakfast pipe, and watched her as she stood the gun against the wall, before walking through the open window of the drawing-room.

Then ten minutes later he joined the little party and found Mrs Stedman beaming, for Alma had come in a penitent mood. She turned to Pretoria Smith as he entered the room and advanced toward him with a smile and an outstretched hand.

"I am very sorry I made such a fool of myself yesterday," she said. "I hope you're going to forget and forgive."

He ignored the hand but smiled into her eyes.

"I owe you an apology, surely," he said lightly, and Marjorie watching the play felt a little chill which sent a shiver down her spine.

What it all meant she could not guess, for her husband was in as genial a mood as Alma, joked with her, rallied her gently upon her stage career and her passion for dramatic situations. When they went out in the garden she followed and saw Lady Tynewood take up her gun.

"Why the lethal weapon?" asked Pretoria Smith.

"Rabbits," she said laconically. "They're rather a nuisance. They get into the garden and destroy my beautiful borders."

Then the girl saw and curled up with the horror of it. The gun that was handled so carelessly by Lady Tynewood was pointed straight at Pretoria Smith's heart and both hammers were raised.

If Pretoria Smith saw this he did not move.

"I don't like rabbits," said Lady Tynewood, and pulled both triggers.

There was a double click and she dropped the gun in her terror. Pretoria Smith looked at the haggard face and the wild eyes and smiled.

"I took the liberty of extracting both cartridges before I came into the drawing-room, Lady Tynewood," he said cheerfully. "I don't like to see loaded guns knocking about."

"It was an accident," she gasped.

"Nearly an accident," Pretoria Smith continued to smile. "And do you know I am almost sympathizing with you at this moment, for you're in a very tight corner, Alma Javot."

Her lips were working convulsively. She could not control them.

"No tighter than yours," she said at last in a low voice.

"Talk it over with Javot," said Pretoria Smith as softly, and turned on his heel.

Marjorie followed him back to the drawing-room.

"She tried to shoot you," she said breathlessly. "She came here to do it!"

"Oh no," said Pretoria Smith as he patted her shoulder gently. "You're distressing yourself unnecessarily. You grow more and more like your mother every day."

Her lips twitched.

"You said that to annoy me and bring me back to sanity," she said, "but she tried, didn't she?"

He nodded.

"I rather fancy she did, poor woman," he said. "I owed her a grudge, but really I have no sense of hatred or malice in my mind. Consider the temptation to her," he said. "I am not talking about the temptation to shoot me, but the temptation to marry that poor boy."

"You called her Alma Javot! What did you mean?"

"She is Javot's wife, and when she married – my brother, she committed bigamy," said Pretoria Smith.

"Then – then he was your brother?"

He nodded.

"I am prepared to continue her income and I think I had better send a note over to that effect before she does something desperate."

"You're prepared?" she gasped. "Why, what do you mean?"

"I mean I am James Tynewood," he said calmly, and she staggered.

He thought she was going to faint and his arm was round her in an instant.

"I think I'll sit down," she said unsteadily. "This has been rather an exciting day."

"You won't topple over or do anything of that kind, will you?" he asked anxiously.

"Not – not if you keep your arm round me," she said.

He leant over to her.

"If I kissed you," he said quietly, "would the blood surge to your head and would you spring up in indignation, or would you faint?"

"I'm curious to know," she said in a smothered voice. "Won't you please try?"

SIR JAMES TYNEWOOD SPEAKS

"I have always been, from my youth up, rather a wanderer," said Pretoria Smith. "I succeeded to the baronetcy when I was a boy of seventeen and still at Eton, and I practically left Eton for Africa and seldom returned. I was an enthusiastic game shot in those days and I grudged the time I had to spend at home. My mother married again after my father's death and she had a son, Norman Garrick, Sir John Garrick being her second husband.

"Norman was always a wild sort of kid, but I was rather fond of him, and when mother died she made me promise that I would look after him and keep him out of mischief. Her husband predeceased her by twelve months," explained Pretoria Smith, "and the boy was left in my charge. I can't say that I carried out my mother's wishes to the letter. I suppose it was selfishness on my part and a desire to satisfy my own fancies and wishes that took me so much out of England and left the boy practically to his own devices.

"I don't know how it happened, but Norman, who had a curious streak of vanity in his composition, must have got mixed up with this fast theatrical set and must have either been introduced or described himself as Sir James Tynewood. He could do this more safely because very few people knew me. I spent such a lot of time abroad, and more people knew Norman, who had been educated on the continent and was as rarely at home as I. Poor old Norman went the pace. He spent more than his allowance. He – he forged my name." Pretoria Smith hesitated. "Yes, I had better tell the truth. He practically robbed the estate of a hundred thousand pounds, a great deal of which went into the pocket of that adventuress, Alma Trebizond as she calls herself, but Alma Javot as she really is.

"Mr Vance, my lawyer, discovered this was going on and that Norman was impersonating me, and sent him a letter by you, which was an extraordinary coincidence – to tell him that I was returning home on the morrow and that he had better drop his friends and retire to the country. But Vance had warned him before and he thought that this was another false alarm.

"What method they employed to induce him to marry Alma Trebizond I do not know, but he certainly was married at the registry office, and then the newspapers came out with the story. The first thing I knew about the marriage was when the *Balmoral Castle* arrived in Southampton. I had been to South Africa on a hunting trip and had taken with me poor Fordham, who was my best friend. Fordham brought me the evening paper and pointed out the item, and we both guessed just what had happened. I hardly knew what to do. We registered at the Grand Western Hotel. I registered myself in my brother's name, because obviously, with the publicity which the marriage had received, if I had registered in my own name the story would have been out and the fraud would have been discovered.

"I came straight to London – you saw me. The next afternoon I went to Tynewood Chase. In the meantime Alma had read the newspapers and had seen in one of them a reference to the Tynewood collar, which is a famous heirloom of ours, and her cupidity being aroused, she demanded from the boy that he should get that collar without delay. The collar, as a matter of fact, is at my bankers, but poor Norman was under the impression that it was in the safe in my study at Tynewood Chase, and he went down immediately to Tynewood and was in the act of smashing up the panels which hide the safe when Fordham and I arrived. I had arranged to meet Norman in London, but he did not keep his appointment. I think he had some desperate idea of getting the collar and bolting with Alma.

"We had a little argument, which was not heated on my side, I am happy to think, and then Norman broke down and told the whole grisly truth, the truth about the defalcations, about his marriage and about his other follies. Whilst we were talking there was an interruption. Somebody came to the door – there were no servants in the house to answer the knock and Fordham went, to admit you.

"When Fordham came back he found me bending over poor Norman, who was sitting at a table, his head upon his hands. I think the revolver must have been in his hand at that moment, for before I could realize or understand what was happening, there was a shot and he collapsed on the floor.

"I felt then that my reproaches had driven him to this act – you heard me say as much. Fordham was splendid. He jeopardized his professional career by giving a certificate that the boy had died a natural death, and he was buried in the chapel, as you probably know.

"There was nothing for me to do but to leave at once and do my best to preserve Norman's secret. From that day I was dead. I saw Vance and arranged to give the woman an income on condition she was not allowed inside the Chase, and I left the next day for South Africa. And that's about the whole of the story," he said, "except that you know how I wandered around at the Cape and how I came to know your uncle."

She was looking at him, big-eyed, and never once did she interrupt him until he finished, then she drew a long sigh.

"Sir James Tynewood," she said, "how wonderful! But who was Jot? Do you remember the name?"

"I am Jot," he smiled. "Those are my initials. James Oliver Tynewood. I was called Jot at Eton and I was always Jot to poor Norman. You ought to have guessed it too."

"Guessed you were Sir James? How?" she asked in surprise.

"Do you not know that it is a tradition of our family that none marry in our chapel but a Tynewood?"

She nodded.

"It is very, very wonderful," she said, "I can't quite grasp it yet."

"Your ladyship will grasp it sooner or later," he said, and she coloured.

"My ladyship?" she repeated. "Oh, of course I'm – "

"You're Lady Tynewood," said "Pretoria Smith."

"I'm dazed – dazed – "

He chuckled quietly.

"Do you think if I kissed you again it would clear all the cobwebs from your brain and make you feel and see all things plainly?"

"I don't know," she said faintly, "but you can try."

THE END

Alma Javot received Sir James Tynewood's letter and wept. If she was repentant, her repentance took a characteristic form.

"It is very decent of him," she said to Javot, "but I'm going to London and back to the stage. It'll look rather good on the bills, Alma, Lady Tynewood."

"You'll get yourself pinched yet," said Javot, "and you'll call yourself Alma Trebizond or I'll come after you."

There was a glint in Mr Javot's eyes which she had seen before.

"Anyway, I'm not going to stay here," she said. "If I can't be Lady Tynewood of Tynewood, I'm not going to be Mrs Javot of Tynewood."

"You can be Mrs Javot of Kensington, if you like," said her placid husband, "and so long as you behave yourself there'll be no kicks coming. I'm staying here to look after the pigs. You can come down and spend your weekends respectably."

She looked at him in surprise.

"You're getting rather soft in your old age, aren't you, Javot?"

"Come any of your monkey tricks and you'll find out," said Mr Javot with a deadly smile. "No, Alma, I've found the life to suit me, looking after the pork, watching the bees and trimming the roses. This is the life."

"Not the life for me," said Alma.

"It will be from Saturday to Monday," said Mr Javot, and his wife agreed, but only after a struggle.

Mrs Stedman had a grievance. She had discovered in her son-in-law a baronet of the United Kingdom and had planned herself a suite in the east wing of Tynewood Chase.

"There is no east wing, mother dear," said Marjorie. "The place is built north and south, and besides, dear – " she did not find it easy to say – "I am not going to live there."

"Not going to live there?" said Mrs Stedman in amazement. "My dear child, are you mad?"

"My husband is going back to South Africa."

"And leave you? Nonsense," said Mrs Stedman, "I'll talk to him!"

"You'll do nothing of the kind, mother," said the girl quietly. "I will manage my own domestic affairs without any assistance."

Mrs Stedman's eyes filled with tears.

"I see," she said bitterly, "my own child has turned against me. She has taken the side of her husband!"

"Don't be ridiculous, mother," said the girl with a little laugh. "I'm not taking his side at all. He's going back to South Africa, and so I shan't live at the Chase. Shall I, James?"

"Jim sounds better to me," said Sir James Tynewood, who had entered the room at that moment. "No, we shan't live at the Chase for weeks and months yet, and I've cancelled my trip to South Africa. You don't mind my staying on here, Mrs Stedman?"

"I should dearly love you to stay, Sir James," said his mother-in-law.

"And perhaps later," said Sir James Tynewood, "you will come along and stay with us at the Chase. We have an east wing commanding a lovely view of the country, and if we haven't got it, we'll build it," he said, and Mrs Stedman glanced triumphantly at her daughter.

"You heard," challenged the girl when her mother had left the room.

"Of course I heard. I spend my life listening at doors," said James Tynewood lazily.

"And you're not going to South Africa?"

"I am going to stay here – right here," said Jim.

There was a pause.

"How long will it be before the Chase is ready?" she asked.

"Weeks and weeks," said Jim cheerfully. "You are sure that your mother doesn't mind my being here?"

"She rather loves having a real baronet in the house," said the girl. "But isn't your room very damp?"

"No, not noticeably," he said in surprise. "I've never seen the slightest vestige of damp."

"Isn't it awfully uncomfortable?" she asked.

"Most comfortable," he replied. "I have never complained."

"Don't you sometimes feel as if you'd like to get up and make some tea at an electric stove?" she asked desperately.

James Tynewood smiled into her eyes and pinched her ear.

"Let's," he said.

Edgar Wallace

Big Foot

Footprints and a dead woman bring together Superintendent Minton and the amateur sleuth Mr Cardew. Who is the man in the shrubbery? Who is the singer of the haunting Moorish tune? Why is Hannah Shaw so determined to go to Pawsy, 'a dog lonely place' she had previously detested? Death lurks in the dark and someone must solve the mystery before BIG FOOT strikes again, in a yet more fiendish manner.

Bones In London

The new Managing Director of Schemes Ltd has an elegant London office and a theatrically dressed assistant – however, Bones, as he is better known, is bored. Luckily there is a slump in the shipping market and it is not long before Joe and Fred Pole pay Bones a visit. They are totally unprepared for Bones' unnerving style of doing business, unprepared for his unique style of innocent and endearing mischief.

EDGAR WALLACE

BONES OF THE RIVER

'Taking the little paper from the pigeon's leg, Hamilton saw it was from Sanders and marked URGENT. *Send Bones instantly to Lujamalababa… Arrest and bring to headquarters the witch doctor.*'

It is a time when the world's most powerful nations are vying for colonial honour, a time of trading steamers and tribal chiefs. In the mysterious African territories administered by Commissioner Sanders, Bones persistently manages to create his own unique style of innocent and endearing mischief.

THE DAFFODIL MYSTERY

When Mr Thomas Lyne, poet, poseur and owner of Lyne's Emporium insults a cashier, Odette Rider, she resigns. Having summoned detective Jack Tarling to investigate another employee, Mr Milburgh, Lyne now changes his plans. Tarling and his Chinese companion refuse to become involved. They pay a visit to Odette's flat and in the hall Tarling meets Sam, convicted felon and protégé of Lyne. Next morning Tarling discovers a body. The hands are crossed on the breast, adorned with a handful of daffodils.

EDGAR WALLACE

THE JOKER
(USA: THE COLOSSUS)

While the millionaire Stratford Harlow is in Princetown, not only does he meet with his lawyer Mr Ellenbury but he gets his first glimpse of the beautiful Aileen Rivers, niece of the actor and convicted felon Arthur Ingle. When Aileen is involved in a car accident on the Thames Embankment, the driver is James Carlton of Scotland Yard. Later that evening Carlton gets a call. It is Aileen. She needs help.

THE SQUARE EMERALD
(USA: THE GIRL FROM SCOTLAND YARD)

'Suicide on the left,' says Chief Inspector Coldwell pleasantly, as he and Leslie Maughan stride along the Thames Embankment during a brutally cold night. A gaunt figure is sprawled across the parapet. But Coldwell soon discovers that Peter Dawlish, fresh out of prison for forgery, is not considering suicide but murder. Coldwell suspects Druze as the intended victim. Maughan disagrees. If Druze dies, she says, 'It will be because he does not love children!'

Printed in Great Britain
by Amazon